ISBN 978-1-331-65838-2
PIBN 10219061

1 MONTH OF
FREE
READING

at

www.ForgottenBooks.com

By purchasing this book you are eligible for one month membership to ForgottenBooks.com, giving you unlimited access to our entire collection of over 700,000 titles via our web site and mobile apps.

To claim your free month visit:
www.forgottenbooks.com/free219061

English
Français
Deutsche
Italiano
Español
Português

www.forgottenbooks.com

Mythology Photography **Fiction**
Fishing Christianity **Art** Cooking
Essays Buddhism Freemasonry
Medicine **Biology** Music **Ancient**
Egypt Evolution Carpentry Physics
Dance Geology **Mathematics** Fitness
Shakespeare **Folklore** Yoga Marketing
Confidence Immortality Biographies
Poetry **Psychology** Witchcraft
Electronics Chemistry History **Law**
Accounting **Philosophy** Anthropology
Alchemy Drama Quantum Mechanics
Atheism Sexual Health **Ancient History**
Entrepreneurship Languages Sport
Paleontology Needlework Islam
Metaphysics Investment Archaeology
Parenting Statistics Criminology
Motivational

ROUGH AND READY;

OR,

LIFE AMONG THE NEW YORK NEWSBOYS.

BY

HORATIO ALGER, Jr.,

AUTHOR OF "RAGGED DICK," "FAME AND FORTUNE," "MARK, THE MATCH
BOY," "CAMPAIGN SERIES," "LUCK AND PLUCK SERIES," ETC.

PHILADELPHIA:
PORTER & COATES.

FAMOUS ALGER BOOKS.

Illustrated, Cloth, Extra, Black and Gold.

RAGGED DICK SERIES. Complete in six vols. **Price per vol., $1 25.**

Ragged Dick, or, Street Life in New York
Fame and Fortune, or, The Progress of Richard Hunter.
Mark the Match Boy
Rough and Ready, or, Life among the New York Newsboys.
Ben the Luggage-Boy, or, Among the Wharves
Rufus and Rose, or, The Fortunes of Rough and Ready.

TATTERED TOM SERIES A Continuation of the Ragged Dick Series.
Price per vol., $1 25.

First Series. Complete in four vols.

Tattered Tom; or, The Story of a Street Arab.
Paul the Peddler, or, The Adventures of a Young Street Merchant.
Phil the Fiddler; or, The Young Street Musician.
Slow and Sure; or, From the Sidewalk to the Shop.

Second Series. Complete in four vols.

Julius; or, The Street Boy out West
The Young Outlaw, or, Adrift in the World.
Sam's Chance, and How he Improved It.
The District Telegraph Boy.

CAMPAIGN SERIES. Complete in three vols. **Price per vol., $1 25.**

Frank's Campaign.
Paul Prescott's Charge.
Charlie Codman's Cruise

LUCK AND PLUCK SERIES. Price per vol., $1 50.

First Series Complete in four vols.

Luck and Pluck; or, John Oakley's Inheritance.
Sink or Swim, or, Harry Raymond's Resolve
Strong and Steady; or, Paddle your Own Canoe.
Strive and Succeed, or, The Progress of Walter Conrad.

Second Series Complete in four vols.

Try and Trust, or, The Story of a Bound Boy.
Bound to Rise, or, How Harry Walton Rose in the World.
Risen from the Ranks, or, Harry Walton's Success.
Herbert Carter's Legacy, or, The Inventor's Son.

BRAVE AND BOLD SERIES. Complete in four vols. Price per vol., $1 50.

Brave and Bold, or, The Story of a Factory Boy.
Jack's Ward, or, The Boy Guardian
Shifting for Himself, or, Gilbert Greyson's Fortunes.
Wait and Hope, or, Ben Bradford's Motto

PACIFIC SERIES. Complete in four vols. **Price per vol., $1 25.**

The Young Adventurer, or, Tom's Trip across the Plains.
The Young Miner, or, Tom Nelson in California.
The Young Explorers; or, Among the Sierras

(Fourth volume in preparation)

Dedication.

---◆---

TO MY DEAR FRIEND,

Theodore Seligman,

THIS VOLUME

IS AFFECTIONATELY DEDICATED.

PREFACE.

"ROUGH AND READY" is presented to the public as the fourth volume of the "Ragged Dick Series," and, like two of its predecessors, was contributed as a serial to the "Schoolmate," a popular juvenile magazine. Its second title, "Life among the New York Newsboys," describes its character and purpose. While the young hero may be regarded as a favorable example of his class, the circumstances of his lot, aggravated by the persecutions of an intemperate parent, are unfortunately too common, as any one at all familiar with the history of the neglected street children in our cities will readily acknowledge.

If "Rough and Ready" has more virtues and fewer faults than most of his class, his history will at least teach the valuable lesson that honesty and good principles are not incompatible even with the greatest social disadvantages, and will, it is hoped, serve as an incentive and stimulus to the young people who may read it.

NEW YORK, Dec. 26, 1869.

ROUGH AND READY;

LIFE AMONG THE NEW YORK NEWSBOYS

——◦◦◦◦——

CHAPTER I.

INTRODUCES ROUGH AND READY.

On the sidewalk in front of the "Times" office, facing Printing-House Square, stood a boy of fifteen, with a pile of morning papers under his arm.

" 'Herald,' 'Times,' 'Tribune,' 'World'!" he vociferated, with a quick glance at each passer-by.

There were plenty of newsboys near by, but this boy was distinguished by his quick, alert movements, and his evident capacity for business. He could tell by a man's looks whether he wanted a paper, and oftentimes a shrewd observation enabled him to judge which of the great morning dailies would be likely to suit the taste of the individual he addressed.

"Here's the 'Tribune,' sir," he said to a tall, thin

9

man, with a carpet-bag and spectacles, who had the appearance of a country clergyman. "Here's the 'Tribune,' — best paper in the city."

"I'm glad you think so, my lad. You may give me one. It's a good sign when a young lad like you shows that he has already formed sound political opinions."

"That's so," said the newsboy.

"I suppose you've seen Horace Greeley?"

"In course, sir, I see him msot every day. He's a brick!"

"A what?" inquired the clergyman, somewhat shocked.

"A brick!"

"My lad, you should not use such a term in speaking of one of the greatest thinkers of the times."

"That's what I mean, sir; only brick's the word we newsboys use."

"It's a low word, my lad; I hope you'll change it. Can you direct me to French's Hotel?"

"Yes, sir; there it is, just at the corner of Frankfort Street."

"Thank you. I live in the country, and am not very well acquainted with New York."

"I thought so"

"Indeed! What made you think so?" asked the clergyman, with a glance of inquiry, unaware that his country air caused him to differ from the denizens of the city.

"By your carpet-bag," said the boy, not caring to mention any other reason.

"What's your name, my lad?"

"Rough and Ready, sir."

"What name did you say?" asked the clergyman, thinking he had not heard aright.

"Rough and Ready, sir."

"That's a singular name."

"My right name is Rufus; but that's what the boys call me."

"Ah, yes, indeed. Well, my lad, I hope you will continue to cherish sound political sentiments until the constitution gives you the right to vote."

"Yes, sir, thank you. — Have a paper, sir?"

The clergyman moved off, and Rough and Ready addressed his next remark to a sallow-complexioned

man, with a flashing black eye, and an immense flap
ping wide-awake hat.

"Paper, sir? Here's the 'World'!"

"Give me a copy. What's that, — the 'Tribune'!
None of your Black Republican papers for me
Greeley's got nigger on the brain. Do you sell many
'Tribunes'?"

"Only a few, sir. The 'World''s the paper! I
only carry the 'Tribune' to accommodate a few cus
tomers."

"I wouldn't have anything to do with it." And
the admirer of the "World" passed on.

"Got the 'Herald'?" inquired the next man.

"Yes, sir, here it is. Smartest paper in the city!
Got twice as much news as all the rest of the papers."

"That's where you're right. Give me the 'Herald'
for my money. It's the most enterprising paper in
America."

"Yes, sir. James Gordon Bennett's a perfect
steam-engine!"

"Ever see him?"

"Yes, sir, often. He's a brick!"

"I believe you."

"Paper, sir? 'Tribune,' sir?"

Rough and Ready addressed this question somewhat doubtfully to a carefully dressed and somewhat
portly gentleman, who got out of a Fourth Avenue
car, and crossed to the sidewalk where he was stand
ing.

"Don't want the 'Tribune.' It's a little too extreme for me. Got the 'Times'?"

"Yes, sir. Here it is. Best paper in the city!"

"I am glad you think so. It's a sound, dignified
journal, in my opinion."

"Yes, sir. That's what I think. Henry J. Raymond's a brick!"

"Ahem, my lad. You mean the right thing, no
doubt; but it would be better to say that he is a
man of statesman-like views."

"That's what I mean, sir. Brick's the word we
newsboys use."

Just then a boy somewhat larger than Rough and
Ready came up. He was stout, and would have been
quite good-looking, if he had been neatly dressed,
and his face and hands had been free from dirt. But
Johnny Nolan, with whom such of my readers as

have read " Ragged Dick " and " Fame and Fortune"
are already acquainted, was not very much troubled
by his deficiencies in either respect, though on the
whole he preferred whole garments, but not enough
to work for them.

Johnny was walking listlessly, quite like a gentleman of leisure.

" How are you, Johnny?" asked Rough and
Ready. " Where's your blacking-box?"

" Somebody stole it," said Johnny, in an aggrieved
tone.

" Why don't you get another?"

" I aint got any money."

" I never knew you when you did have," said the
newsboy.

" I aint lucky," said Johnny.

" You won't be till you're a little smarter than you
are now. What are you going to do?"

" I dunno," said Johnny. " I wish Mr. Taylor
was in this city."

" What for?"

" He used to give me money most every day," said
Johnny.

" I don't want anybody to give me money," said Rough and Ready, independently. " I can earn my own living."

" I could get a place to tend a paper-stand, if I had good clo'es," said Johnny.

" Why don't you go to work and earn enough money to buy some, then?" said the newsboy.

" I can't. I aint got no money."

" I've sold sixty papers this morning, and made sixty cents," said Rough and Ready.

" I aint made nothing," said Johnny, despondently.

" Come, I'll tell you what I'll do," said the news-boy. " Here's two ' Tribunes,' two ' Worlds' and ' Times ' and three ' Heralds.' Just go round the cor-ner, and sell 'em, and I'll give you all the profits."

" All right! " said Johnny, brightening up at the prospect of making something. " What's the news?"

" Steamboat exploded on the Mississippi! Five hundred people thrown half a mile high in the air! One man miraculously saved by falling in a mud-hole! Can you remember all that?"

" Yes," said Johnny. " Give me the papers."

Johnny went round to Nassau Street, and began **to** cry the remarkable news which had just been communicated to him.

"That ought to sell the papers," said Rough and Ready to himself. "Anyway, Johnny's got it exclu sive. There aint any other newsboy that's got it."

In about half an hour Johnny came back empty handed.

"Sold all your papers?" asked the newsboy.

"Yes," said Johnny; "but was that true about **the** steamboat?"

"Why?"

"'Cause people looked for it, and couldn't **find** it, and one man said he'd give me a lickin' if I called out news that wasn't true."

"Well, if it isn't true now, it will be some other day. Explosions is a permanent institution. Anyhow, it isn't any worse for us to cry news that aint true, than for the papers to print it when they know it's false."

Whatever may be thought of the morality of Rough and Ready's views on this subject, it must be admitted that in manufacturing news to make his papers sell, he was only imitating the example of some of our most prominent publishers. The same may be said of his readiness to adopt the political views and prejudices of his customers, for commercial profit. I may as well remark here, that, though Rough and Ready is a favorite of mine, for his energy, enterprise, and generous qualities, I do not mean to represent him as a model boy. I shall probably have to record some things of him which I cannot wholly approve. But then it is to be considered that he is a newsboy, whose advantages have been limited, who has been a familiar witness to different forms of wickedness ever since he was old enough to notice anything, and, notwithstanding, has grown up to be a pretty good boy, though not a model.

In fact, one reason why I do not introduce any model boys into my stories is that I do not find them in real life. I know a good many of various degrees of goodness; but most of them have more failings than one, — failings which are natural to boys, springing oftentimes more from thoughtlessness than actual perverseness. These faults they must struggle with, and by determined effort they

2

will be able, with God's help, to overcome them They have less excuse than the friendless newsboy, because more care has been bestowed upon their education and moral training.

" Here's eleven cents, Johnny," said the newsboy, after receiving from his assistant the proceeds of his sales. "Isn't it better to earn them than have somebody give them to you?" '

" I dunno," said Johnny, doubtfully.

" Well, you ought to, then.   I've sold fifteen more. That's seventy-five I've sold this morning.   What are you going to do with your money?"

" I got trusted for breakfast at the Lodge this mornin'," said Johnny ; " but I must earn some more money, or I can't buy any dinner."

" Which do you like best, — selling papers, or blacking boots?"

" I like blackin' boots.   'Taint so hard work.

" Why didn't you take care of your box?"

" I laid it down in a doorway.   I guess some boy stole it."

" I'll tell you what I'll do, Johnny.   I'll buy you a new box and brush, and we'll go *whacks*."

" All right, " said Johnny.

As the allusion may not be understood by some of my young readers, I will explain that it is a custom among the more enterprising street boys, who are capitalists to a small amount, to set up their more needy fellows in business, on condition that they will pay half their earnings to the said capitalists as a profit on the money advanced. This is called " going whacks." It need hardly be said that it is a very profitable operation to the young capitalist, often paying fifty per cent. daily on his loan, — a transaction which quite casts into the shade the most tempting speculations of Wall Street.

It is noteworthy that these young Bohemians, lawles as they often are, have a strict code of honor in regard to such arrangements, and seldom fail to make honest returns, setting a good example in so far to older business operators.

On receiving Johnny's assent to his proposal, the newsboy proceeded to a street stand on Nassau Street, and bought the necessary articles for his companion, and then the two separated.

Johnny, confiding in his prospects of future profits.

stopped at the pie and cake stand at the north-east
corner of Nassau and Fulton Streets, and bought of
the enterprising old woman who has presided over it
for a score of years, a couple of little pies, which he
ate with a good appetite. He then shouldered his
box and went to business.

CHAPTER II.

LITTLE ROSE.

ROUGH AND READY had sold out his stock of morn-ing papers, and would have no more to do until the afternoon, when the "Evening Post" and "Express" appeared. The "Mail," "Telegram," and "News," which now give employment to so many boys, were not then in existence.

I may as well take this opportunity to describe the newsboy who is to be the hero of my present story. As already mentioned, he was fifteen years old, stoutly built, with a clear, fresh complexion, and a resolute, good-humored face. He was independent and self-reliant, feeling able to work his own way without help, and possessed a tact and spirit of en-terprise which augured well for his success in life. Though not so carefully dressed as most of the boys who will read this story, he was far from being as ragged as many of his fellow-newsboys. There were two reasons for this :·he had a feeling of pride, which made him take some care of his clothes, and besides, until within a year, he had had a mother to look after him. In this respect he had an advantage over the homeless boys who wander about the streets, not knowing where they shall find shelter.

But, within a year, circumstances had changed with our young hero. His mother had been left a widow when he was nine years old. Two years later she married a man, of whom she knew comparatively little, not from love, but chiefly that she might secure a comfortable support for her two children. This man, Martin, was a house-carpenter, and was chiefly employed in Brooklyn and New York. He removed his new wife and the children from the little Connecticut village, where they had hitherto lived, to New York, where he found lodgings for them.

In the course of a few months, she found that the man she had so hastily married had a violent, and even brutal, temper, and was addicted to intemperate habits, which were constantly interfering with his prospects of steady employment. Instead of her care and labor being lessened, both were increased

The lodgings to which Martin carried his wife, at first, were respectable, but after a while there was a diffi-culty about the rent, and they were obliged to move. They moved frequently, each time compelled to take dirtier and shabbier accommodations.

Rufus was soon taken from school, and compelled, as a newsboy, to do his part towards supporting the family. In fact, his earnings generally amounted to more than his stepfather's, who only worked irreg-ularly. A year before the date of our story, Mrs. Martin died, solemnly intrusting to her son the charge of his little sister Rose, then six years old.

"Take good care of her," said the dying mother. "You know what your stepfather is. Don't let him beat or ill-treat her. I trust her wholly to you."

"I'll take care of her, mother," said Rufus, stur-dily. "Don't be afraid for her."

"God will help you, Rufus," said the poor mother "I am glad you are such a boy as I can trust."

"I aint so good as I might be, mother," said Rufus, touched by the scene; "but you can trust me with Rosie."

Mrs. Martin knew that Rufus was a sturdy and

self-relying boy, and she felt that she could trust him
So her last moments were more peaceful than the,
would have been but for this belief.

After her death, Rufus continued the main support
of the household. He agreed to pay the rent, — five
dollars monthly, — and fifty cents a day towards the
purchase of food. This he did faithfully. He found
himself obliged, besides, to buy clothing for his little
sister, for his stepfather, who spent his time chiefly in
bar-rooms, troubled himself very little about the little
girl, except to swear at her when he was irritated.

Rough and Ready gained his name partly from its
resemblance in sound to his right name of Rufus, but
chiefly because it described him pretty well. Any of
his street associates, who attempted to impose upon
him, found him a rough customer. He had a pair of
strong arms, and was ready to use them when occa-
sion seemed to require it. But he was not quarrelsome. He was generous and kind to smaller boys,
and was always willing to take their part against
those who tried to take advantage of their weakness
There was a certain Tom Price, a big, swaggering
street-bully, a boot black by profession, with whom

Rough and Ready had had more than one sharp con-
test, which terminated in his favor, though a head
shorter than his opponent.

To tell the truth, Rough and Ready, in addition to
his strength, had the advantage of a few lessons in
boxing, which he had received from a young man who
had been at one time an inmate of the same building
with himself. This knowledge served him in good
stead.

I hope my young readers will not infer that I am
an advocate of fighting. It can hardly help being
brutal under any circumstances ; but where it is never
resorted to except to check ruffianism, as in the case
of my young hero, it is less censurable.

After setting up Johnny Nolan in business, Rough
and Ready crossed to the opposite side of the street,
and walked up Centre Street. He stopped to buy a
red-checked apple at one of the old women's stalls
which he passed.

" Rosie likes apples," he said to himself. " I suppose she's waiting to hear me come upstairs."

He walked for about quarter of a mile, till he came
in sight of the Tombs, which is situated at the north

west corner of Centre and Leonard Streets, fronting on the first. It is a grim-looking building, built of massive stone. Rough and Ready did not quite go up to it, but turned off, and went down Leonard Street in an easterly direction.

Leonard Street, between Centre and Baxter Streets, is wretched and squalid, not as bad perhaps as some of the streets in the neighborhood, — for example, Baxter Street, — but a very undesirable residence.

Here it was, however, that our hero and his sister lived. It was not his own choice, for he would have gladly lived in a neat, clean street; but he could not afford to pay a high rent, and so was compelled to remain where he was.

He paused in front of a dilapidated brick building of six stories. The bricks were defaced, and the blinds were broken, and the whole building looked miserable and neglected. There was a grocery shop kept in the lower part, and the remaining five stories were crowded with tenants, two or three families to a floor. The street was generally littered up with old wagons, in a broken-down condition, and odors far from savory rose from the garbage that was piled up here and there.

Crowds of pale, unhealthy-looking children, with dirty faces, generally bare-headed and bare-footed, played about, managing, with the happy faculty of childhood, to show light-hearted gayety, even under the most unpromising circumstances.

Rough and Ready, who was proud of his little sister, liked to have her appear more decently clad than most of the children in the street. Little Rose never appeared without a bonnet, and both shoes and stockings, and through envy of her more respectable appearance, some of the street girls addressed her with mock respect, as Miss Rose. But no one dared to treat her otherwise than well, when her brother was near, as his prowess was well known throughout the neighborhood.

Our hero dashed up the dark and rickety stair case, two stairs at a time, ascending from story to story, until he stood on the fifth landing.

A door was eagerly opened, and a little girl of seven called out joyfully : —

" Is it you, Rufus ? "

At home, Rough and Ready dropped his street nickname, and was known by his proper appellation.

" Yes, Rosie. Did you get tired of waiting?"

" I'm always tired of waiting. The mornings seem so long."

" Yes, it must seem long to you. Did **you** go **out** and play?"

" Only a few minutes."

" Didn't you want to stay?"

The little girl looked embarrassed.

" I went out a little while, but the girls kept calling me Miss Rose, and I came in."

" I'd like to hear 'em ! " said Rufus, angrily.

" They don't do it when you are here. They don't dare to," said Rose, looking with pride at her brother, whom she looked upon as a young hero.

" They'd better not," said the newsboy, significantly. " They'd wish they hadn't, that's all."

" You see I wore my new clothes," said Rose, by way of explanation. " That made them think I was proud, and putting on airs. But they won't do it again."

" Why not? " asked her brother, puzzled.

"Because," said Rose, sadly, "I shan't wear them again."

"Shan't wear them!" repeated Rough and Ready. "Are you afraid to?"

"I can't."

"Why can't you?"

"Because I haven't got them to wear."

Rose's lip quivered as she said this, and she looked ready to cry.

"I don't understand you, Rosie," said the newsboy, looking perplexed. "Why haven't you got them, I should like to know?"

"Because father came home, and took them away," said the little girl.

"*What!*" exclaimed Rough and Ready, quickly. "Took them away?"

"Yes."

"What did he do that for?" said the boy, angrily.

"He said he shouldn't let you waste your money in buying nice clothes for me. He said that my old ones were good enough."

"When did he take them away?" said the boy, his heart stirred with indignation.

" Only a little while ago."

" Do you know where he took them, Rosie?"

" He said he was going to take them to Baxter Street to sell. He said he wasn't going to have me dressed out like a princess, while he hadn't a cent of money in his pocket."

Poor Rufus! He had been more than a month saving up money to buy some decent clothes for his little sister. He had economized in every possible way to accomplish it, anticipating her delight when the new hat and dress should be given her. He cared more that she should appear well than himself, for in other eyes, besides her brother's, Rose was a charming little girl. She had the same clear complexion as her brother, an open brow, soft, silken hair hanging in natural curls, fresh, rosy cheeks in spite of the unhealthy tenement-house in which she lived, and a confiding look in her dark blue eyes, which proved very attractive.

Only the day before, the newsboy had brought home the new clothes, and felt abundantly rewarded by the delight of his little sister, and the improvement in her appearance. He had never before seen her looking so well.

But now — he could not think of it without indignation — his intemperate step-father had taken away the clothes which he had worked so hard to buy, and, by this time, had probably sold them for one quarter of their value at one of the old-clothes shops in Baxter Street.

"It's too bad, Rosie!" he said. "I'll go out, and see if I can't get them back."

While he was speaking, an unsteady step was heard on the staircase.

"He's coming!" said Rose, with a terrified look.

A hard and resolute look came into the boy's face, as, turning towards the door, he awaited the entrance of his stepfather.

CHAPTER III.

A SUDDEN MOVE.

PRESENTLY the door was opened, and James **Martin** entered with an unsteady step. His breath was redolent with the fumes of alcohol, and his face wore the brutish, stupid look of one who was under the influence of intoxication. He was rather above the middle height, with a frame originally strong. His hair and beard had a reddish tinge. However he might have appeared if carefully dressed, he certainly presented an appearance far from prepossessing at the present moment.

Rough and Ready surveyed his stepfather with a glance of contempt and disgust, which he did not attempt to conceal. Rose clung to his side with a terrified look.

"What are you doing here?" demanded Martin, sinking heavily into a chair.

"I'm taking care of my sister," said the newsboy, putting his arm protectingly round Rose's neck.

"You'd better go to work. I can take care of her," said the stepfather.

"Nice care you take of her!" retorted the newsboy, indignantly.

"Don't you be impudent, you young rascal," said Martin, with an unsteady voice. "If you are, I'll give you a flogging."

"Don't talk to him, Rufie," said little Rose, who had reason to fear her stepfather.

"I must, Rosie," said the newsboy, in a low voice.

"What are you muttering there?" demanded the drunkard, suspiciously.

"Where are my sister's new clothes?" asked Rough and Ready.

"I don't know about any new clothes. She aint got any as I know of."

"She had some this morning, — some that I bought and paid for. What have you done with them?"

"I've sold 'em," said Martin, doggedly, his assumed

3

ignorance ceasing. " That's what I've done with 'em."

" What did you sell them for ? " demanded the newsboy, persistently.

" What business has she got with new clothes, when we haven't got enough to eat, I'd like to know ? "

" If we haven't got enough to eat, it isn't my fault," said the boy, promptly. "I do my part towards supporting the family. As for you, you spend all your money for rum, and some of mine too."

" What business is it of yours ? " said the drunkard, defiantly.

" I want you to bring back my sister's clothes. What have you done with them ? "

" You're an impudent young rascal."

" That isn't answering my question."

" Do you want me to give you a flogging ? " asked Martin, looking angrily at our hero from his inflamed eyes.

" Don't say any more to him, Rufus," said little Rose, timidly.

" You ought to be ashamed of yourself, stealing a little girl's clothes, and selling them for rum," said the newsboy, scornfully.

This was apparently too much for the temper of Martin, never very good. He rose from his chair, and made a movement towards the newsboy, with the purpose of inflicting punishment upon him for his bold speech. But he had drunk deeply in the morning, and since selling little Rose's clothes, had invested part of the proceeds in additional liquor, which now had its effect. He stood a moment wavering, then made a step forward, but the room seemed to reel about, and he fell forward in the stupor of intoxication. He did not attempt to rise, but lay where he fell, breathing heavily.

" O Rufus ! " cried Rose, clinging still more closely to her brother, whom she felt to be her only protector.

" Don't be afraid, Rosie," said the newsboy. " He won't hurt you. He's too drunk for that."

" But when he gets over it, he'll be so angry, he'll beat me."

" I'd like to see him do it ! " said the newsboy, his eye flashing.

"I'm so afraid of him, Rufus. He wasn't quite so bad when mother was alive. It's awful to live with him."

"You shan't live with him any longer, Rose."

"What do you mean, Rufus?" said the little girl, with an inquiring glance.

"I mean that I'm going to take you away," said the boy, firmly. "You shan't live any longer with such a brute."

"Where can we go, Rufus?"

"I don't know. Any place will be better than here."

"But will he let me go?" asked Rose, with a timid look at the form stretched out at her feet.

"I shan't ask him."

"He will be angry."

"Let him be. We've had enough of him. We'll go away and live by ourselves."

"That will be nice," said little Rose, hopefully "somewhere where he cannot find us."

"Yes, somewhere where he cannot find us."

"When shall we go?"

"Now,' said the newsboy, promptly. "We'll g

while he is lying there, and can't interfere with us. Get your bonnet, and we'll start."

A change of residence with those who have a su-perfluity of this world's goods is a formidable affair. But the newsboy and his sister possessed little or nothing besides what they had on, and a very small bundle, done up hastily in an old paper on which Rough and Ready had been "stuck," that is, which he had left on his hands, contained everything which they needed to take away.

They left the room, closing the door after them, and went down the rickety stairs, the little girl's hand being placed confidingly in that of her brother. At length they reached the foot of the last staircase, and passed through the outer door upon the side-walk.

"It's the last time you'll go into that house," said the newsboy. "You can bid good-by to it."

"Where are we going now, Rufus?"

"I am going to see if I can find, and buy back, your new clothes, Rose. We'll walk along Baxter Street, and maybe we'll see them hanging up in some shop."

"But have you got money enough to buy them back, Rufus?"

"I think I have, Rose. Wouldn't you like to have them again?"

"Yes, Rufus; but it is too much money for you to pay. Never mind the clothes. I can get along without them," said Rose, though it cost her a pang to give up the nice dress which had given her so much innocent pleasure.

"No, Rose, I want you to wear them. We are going to live respectably now, and I don't want to see you wearing that old calico dress."

Little Rose was dressed in a faded calico gown, which had been made over, not very artistically, from a dress which had belonged to her mother. It had been long in use, and showed the effects of long wear. It had for some time annoyed the newsboy, who cared more that his sister should appear well dressed than himself. He knew that his sister was pretty, and he felt proud of her. Feeling as he did, it is no wonder that his indignation was aroused by the conduct of his stepfather in selling his little sister's new clothes, which he had bought out of his scanty earnings.

While they had been speaking, they had walked to the end of the block and turned into Baxter Street.

Baxter Street is one of the most miserable streets in the most miserable quarter of the city. It is lined with old-clothing shops, gambling-dens, tumble-down tenements, and drinking saloons, and at all times it swarms with sickly and neglected children, bold and wretched women, and the lowest class of men. One building, which goes by the name of Monkey Hall, is said to be a boarding-house for the monkeys, which during the day are carried about by Italian organ-grinders. It was in this street where Rufus had reason to believe that his sister's clothes might be found.

The two children walked slowly on the west side, looking into the old-clothes shops, as they passed

" Come in, boy," said a woman at the entrance of one of the shops. " I'll fit you out cheap."

" Have you got any clothes that will do for this little girl ?" asked the newsboy.

" For the little gal ? Yes, come in; I'll fit her **out** like a queen."

The shabby little shop hardly looked like a place

where royal attire could be procured. Still it might be that his sister's clothes had been sold to this woman ; so Rough and Ready thought it well to enter.

The woman rummaged about among some female attire at the back part of the shop, and brought forward a large-figured de laine dress, of dingy appearance, and began to expatiate upon its beauty in a voluble tone.

" That's too large," said Rough and Ready. " It's big enough for me."

" Maybe you'd like it for yourself," said the woman, with a laugh.

" I don't think it would suit my style of beauty," said the newsboy. " Haven't you got anything smaller ? "

" This'll do," persisted the woman. " All you've got to do is to tuck it up so ; " and she indicated the alteration. " I'll sew it up in a minute."

" No, it won't do," said the newsboy, decidedly. " Come, Rose."

They went into another shop, where a man was in attendance ; but here again their inquiries were fruitless.

They emerged from the shop, and, just beyond, came to a basement shop, the entrance to which was lined with old clothes of every style and material. Some had originally been of fine cloth and well made, but had in course of time made their way from the drawing-room to this low cellar. There were clothes of coarser texture and vulgar cut, originally made for less aristocratic customers, which perhaps had been sold to obtain the necessaries of life, or very possibly to procure supplies for the purchase of rum. Looking down into this under-ground shop, the quick eyes of Rose caught sight of the new dress, of which she had been so proud, depending from a nail just inside.

"There it is," she said, touching the newsboy on the arm. "I can see it."

"So it is. Let's go down."

They descended the stone steps, and found them selves in a dark room, about twelve feet square, hung round with second-hand garments. The presiding genius of the establishment was a little old man, with a dirty yellow complexion, his face seamed with wrinkles, but with keen, sharp eyes, who looked like a spider on the watch for flies.

"What can I sell you to-day, young gentleman?" he asked, rubbing his hands insinuatingly.

"What's the price of that dress?" asked Rough and Ready, coming straight to the point.

"That elegant dress," said the old man, "cost me a great deal of money.   It's very fine."

"I know all about it," said the newsboy, "for I bought it for my sister last week."

"No, no, you are mistaken, young gentleman," said the old man, hastily, fearing it was about to be reclaimed.   "I've had it in my shop a month."

"No, you haven't," said the newsboy, bluntly; "you bought it this morning of a tall man, with a red nose."

"How can you say so, young gentleman?"

"Because it's true.   The man took it from my sister, and carried it off.   How much did you pay for it?"

"I gave two dollars and a half," said the old man, judging from the newsboy's tone that it was useless to persist in his denial. " You may have it for three dollars."

" That's too much. I don't believe you gave more than a dollar. I'll give you a dollar and a half."

The old man tried hard to get more, but as Rough and Ready was firm, and, moreover, as he had only given fifty cents for the dress an hour before, he con cluded that he should be doing pretty well in making two hundred per cent. profit, and let it go.

The newsboy at once paid the money, and asked if his sister could put it on there. A door in the back part of the shop was opened, revealing an inner room, where Rose speedily made the change, and emerged into the street with her old dress rolled up in a bundle.

CHAPTER IV.

A FORTUNATE MEETING.

"WHERE are we going, Rufus?" asked Rose, as they left the subterranean shop.

"That's what I'm trying to think, Rose," said her brother, not a little perplexed.

To tell the truth, Rough and Ready had acted from impulse, and without any well-defined plan in his mind. He had resolved to take Rose from her old home, if it deserved the name, and for reasons which the reader will no doubt pronounce sufficient; but he had not yet had time to consider where they should live in future.

This was a puzzling question.

If the newsboy had been a capitalist, or in receipt of a handsome income, the question would have been a very simple one. He would only need to have bought a "Morning Herald," and, from the long list of boarding and lodging houses, have selected one which he judged suitable. But his income was small, and he had himself and his sister to provide for. He knew that it must be lonely for Rose to pass the greater part of the day without him ; yet it seemed to be necessary. If only there was some suitable person for her to be with. The loss of her mother was a great one to Rose, for it left her almost without a companion.

So Rough and Ready knit his brows in perplexing thought.

"I can't tell where we'd better go, Rose, yet," he said at last. "We'll have to look round a little, and perhaps we'll come across some good place."

"I hope it'll be some place where father won't find us," said Rose.

"Don't call him father," said the newsboy, hastily. "He isn't our father."

"No," said Rose, "I know that, — that is not ou own father."

"Do you remember our own father, Rose? But of course you don't, for you were only a year old when he died."

"How old were you, Rufus?"

"I was nine."

"Tell me about father. Mother used to tell me about him sometimes."

"He was always kind and good. I remember his pleasant smile whenever he came home. Once he was pretty well off; but he failed in business, and had to give up his store, and, soon after, he died, so that mother was left destitute. Then she married Mr. Martin."

"What made her?"

"It was for our sake, Rose. She thought he would give us a good home. But you know how it turned out. Sometimes I think mother might have been alive now, if she hadn't married him."

"Oh, I wish she was," said Rose, sighing.

"Well, Rose, we won't talk any more of Mr. Martin. He hasn't got any more to do with us. He can take care of himself, and we will take care of ourselves."

"I don't know, Rufie," said the little girl; "I'm afraid he'll do us some harm."

"Don't be afraid, Rose; I aint afraid of him, and I'll take care he don't touch you."

The little girl's apprehensions were not without good reason. They had not done with this man Martin. He was yet to cause them considerable trouble. What that trouble was will be developed in the course of the story. Our business now is to follow the course of the two orphans.

They had reached and crossed the City Hall Park, and now stood on the Broadway pavement, opposite Murray Street.

"Are we going to cross Broadway, Rufus?" asked his little sister.

"Yes, Rose. I've been thinking you would feel more comfortable to be as far away from our old room as possible. If we can get a lodging on the west side of Broadway somewhere, we shan't be so apt to meet Mr. Martin. You'd like that better, wouldn't you?"

"Oh, yes, I should like that better."

"Now we'll cross. Keep firm hold of my, hand Rose, or you'll get run over."

During the hours of daylight, except on Sunday, there is hardly a pause in the long line of vehicles of every description that make their way up and down

the great central thoroughfare of the city. A quick
eye and a quick step are needed to cross in safety.
But the practised newsboy found no difficulty. Dodg-
ing this way and that, he led his sister safely across.

" Let us go up Broadway, Rufus," said the little
girl, who, living always in the eastern part of the
city, was more used to Chatham Street and the Bowery than the more fashionable Broadway.

" All right, Rose. We can turn off higher up."

So the newsboy walked up Broadway, on the west
side, his little sister clinging to his arm. Occasionally, though they didn't know it, glances of interest
were directed towards them. The attractive face of
little Rose, set off by her neat attire, and the frank,
open countenance of our young hero, who looked
more manly in his character of guardian to his little
sister, made a pleasant impression upon the passers-
by, or at least such as could spare a thought from
the business cares which are apt to engross the mind
to the exclusion of everything.

"If I only had two such children !" thought a child-
less millionnaire, as he passed with a hurried step.
His coffers were full of gold, but his home was

empty of comfort and happiness. He might easily
have secured it by diverting a trifling rill, from his
full stream of riches, to the channel of charity; but
this never entered his mind.

So the children walked up the street, jostled by
hurrying multitudes, little Rose gazing with childish
interest at the shop windows, and the objects they
presented. As for Rough and Ready, Broadway
was no novelty to him. His busy feet had traversed
every portion of the city, or at least the lower part,
and he felt at home everywhere. While his sister
was gazing at the shop windows, he was engaged in
trying to solve the difficult question which was still
puzzling him, — " Where should he find a home for
his sister? "

The solution of the question was nearer than he
anticipated.

As they passed a large clothing-house, the little
girl's attention was suddenly attracted to a young
woman, who came out of the front entrance with a
large bundle under her arm.

" O Miss Manning," she cried, joyfully, " how **do**
you do? "

"What, little Rose!" exclaimed the seamstress, a cordial smile lighting up her face, pale from confinement and want of exercise.

"How are you, Miss Manning?" said the newsboy, in an off-hand manner.

"I am glad to see you, Rufus," said the young woman, shaking hands with him. "How you have grown!"

"Have I?" said Rough and Ready, pleased with what he regarded as a compliment. "I'm glad I'm getting up in the world that way, if I can't in any other."

"Do you sell papers now, Rufus?"

"Yes. I expect all the newspaper editors would fail if I didn't help 'em off with their papers."

"You are both looking fresh and rosy."

"Particularly Rose," said the newsboy, laughing. "But you are not looking very well, Miss Manning."

"Oh, I'm pretty well," said the seamstress; "but I don't get much chance to get out into the air."

"You work too hard."

"I have to work hard," she replied, smiling

faintly. " Sewing is not very well paid, and it costs a great deal to live. Where are you living now?"

" We are not living anywhere," said Rose.

"We are living on Broadway just at present," said Rough and Ready.

The seamstress looked from one to the other in surprise, not understanding what they meant.

" Where is your father now?" she asked.

" I have no father," said the newsboy.

" Is Mr. Martin dead, then?"

"No, he's alive, but he isn't my father, and I won't own him as such. If you want to know where he is, I will tell you. He is lying drunk on the floor of a room on Leonard Street, or at least he was half an hour ago."

The newsboy spoke with some bitterness, for he never could think with any patience of the man who had embittered the last years of his mother's life, and had that very morning nearly deprived his little sister of the clothing which he had purchased for her

" Have you left him, then?" asked the seamstress

" Yes, we have left him, and we do not mean to go near him again."

"Then you mean to take the whole care of your little sister, Rufus?"

"Yes."

"It is a great responsibility for a boy like you."

"It is what I have been doing all along. Mr. Martin hasn't earned his share of the expenses. I've had to take care of us both, and him too, and then he didn't treat us decently. I'll tell you what he did this morning."

Here he told the story of the manner in which his little sister had been robbed of her dress.

"You don't think I'd stand that, Miss Manning. do you?" he said, lifting his eyes to hers.

"No, Rufus; it seemed hard treatment. So you're going to find a home somewhere else?"

"Yes."

"Where do you expect to go?"

"Well, that is what puzzles me," said the news-boy. "I want some place in the west part of the city, so as to be out of Martin's way. Where do you live?"

"In Franklin Street, not far from the river."

"Is it a good place?"

"As good as I can expect. You know that I am poor as well as you."

"Is there any chance for us in the house?" asked Rufus, with a sudden idea touching the solution of the problem that had troubled him.

"No, there is no room vacant, I believe," said the seamstress, thoughtfully. "If there were only Rose, now," she added, "I could take her into the room with me."

"That's just the thing," said Rufus, joyfully. "Rose, wouldn't you like to be with Miss Manning? Then you would have company every day."

"Yes," said Rose, "I should like it ever so much; but where would you be?" she asked, doubtfully.

"I'll go to the Newsboys' Lodging House to sleep, but I'll come every afternoon and evening to see you. I'll give Miss Manning so much a week for your share of the expenses, and then I'll feel easy about you. But wouldn't she be a trouble to you, Miss Manning?"

"A trouble," repeated the seamstress. "You don't know how much I shall enjoy her company. I get so lonely sometimes. If you'll come with me now, I'll show you my room, and Rose shall find a home at once."

Much relieved in mind, Rough and Ready, with his sister still clinging to his arm, followed the seamstress down Franklin Street towards her home near the river.

CHAPTER V.

A NEW HOME.

MISS MANNING paused before a house, not indeed very stylish, but considerably more attractive than the tenement house in Leonard Street.

" This is where I live," she said.

" Is it a tenement house?" asked the newsboy.

" No, there's a woman keeps it, — a Mrs. Nelson. Some of the rooms are occupied by boarders, but others only by lodgers. I can't afford to pay the board she asks; so I only hire a room, and board my self."

While she was speaking, the two children were following her upstairs.

The entries were dark, and the stairs uncarpeted, but neither Rough and Ready nor his sister had been used to anything better, and were far from criticising what might have been disagreeable to those more fastidious.

Miss Manning kept on till she reached the fourth story. Here she paused before a door, and, taking a key from her pocket, opened it.

" This is where I live," she said. " Come in, both of you."

The room occupied by the seamstress was about twelve feet square. Though humble enough in its appearance, it was exquisitely neat. In the centre of the floor was a strip of carpeting about eight feet square, leaving, of course, a margin of bare floor on all sides.

" Why, you've got a carpet, Miss Manning ! " said Rose, with pleasure.

" Yes," said the seamstress, complacently; " I bought it at an auction store one day, for only a dollar and a half. I couldn't well spare the money ; but it seemed so nice to have a carpet, that I yielded to the temptation, and bought it."

" It seems more respectable to have a carpet," said the newsboy.

" It's more comfortable," said Miss Manning, " and it seems as if the room was warmer, although it doesn't cover the whole floor."

" What a nice little stove ! " said Rose, admiringly.
" Can you cook by it ? "

She pointed to a small square stove, at one end of
the apartment.

" Oh, yes, I can boil eggs, and do almost anything.
I bought it at a junk-shop for only two dollars. I
don't have a fire all the time, because I can't afford
it. But it is pleasant, even when I am feeling cold,
to think that I can have a fire when I want to."

In the corner of the room was a bedstead. There
was also a very plain, and somewhat battered, bureau,
and a small glass of seven inches by nine hanging
over it. On a small table were placed half-a-dozen
books, including the Bible, which years ago Miss
Manning had brought from her country home, the gift
of a mother, now many years dead. The poor seamstress never let a day pass without reading a chapter
in the good book, and, among all her trials and priva-
tions, of which she had many, she had never failed to
derive comfort and good cheer from it.

" How nice your room looks, Miss Manning ! " said
Rose, admiringly.

" Yes, it's jolly," said the newsboy.

"I try to make it as comfortable as I can; but **my** means are small, and I cannot do all I wish."

"And are you willing to let Rose come and live with you?"

"I shall be very glad to have her. She will be so much company for me."

"You'd like to come, Rosie, wouldn't you?"

"Ever so much," said the little girl; "that is, **if** I can see you every day."

"Of course you will. I'll come up to see how you're gettin' along."

"Then it's all settled," said the seamstress, cheerfully. "Take off your bonnet, Rose, and I'll tell you where to put it."

"It isn't all settled yet," said Rough and Ready. "I must find out about how much it's going to cost for Rose, and then I can pay you so much every week. How much rent do you pay for this room?"

"It costs me a dollar a week."

"Maybe they'll charge more if there are **two** in it."

"I think not much. I could go and ask Mrs. Nelson."

"I wish you would."

The seamstress went downstairs, and saw the landlady. She returned with the intelligence that Mrs. Nelson would be willing to have her receive Rose on the payment of twenty-five cents additional.

"That will make a dollar and a quarter for the two," said the newsboy. "Then I'll pay sixty-two cents a week for Rose's share."

"No," said the seamstress, — "only twenty-five cents. That is all that is charged extra for her."

"Rose must pay her half of the expenses," said the newsboy, decidedly. "That'll be sixty-two cents a week for the rent."

"But you've got yourself to provide for, as well as your little sister," said the seamstress.

"I can do it," said Rough and Ready, confidently. "Don't you worry about that."

"But it seems as if I was making money out of Rose."

"No more'n she is making money out of you. It's the same for both, as far as I can see," said the newsboy. "Now, how much does it cost you for eatin' a week?"

"About a dollar and a quarter," said the seam stress, after a little thought.

"That's a very little. What can you get for that?"

"There's a small loaf of bread every day. I get that at the baker's round the corner. I don't often get butter, but I keep a little on hand, so that when my appetite is poor I can use it. When eggs are cheap, I boil one for my breakfast."

"Don't you ever eat meat?"

"Sometimes I buy half a pound of steak at the market. That lasts me two days. It strengthens me up wonderfully."

"Half a pound of meat in two days!" repeated Rough and Ready, wonderingly. "I guess you don't know what it is to have a newsboy's appetite."

"No," said the seamstress, smiling. "I never was a newsboy that I remember."

"Rufie can sell papers as fast as anything," said Rose, who had a high appreciation of her brother's merits. "I stood by him one morning when he was selling. He knew just what paper everybody wanted, and made them buy, whether they wanted to or not."

"Oh, I'm a rouser at selling papers," said the newsboy. "I can sell more in a mornin' than any boy on the street."

"You look like a smart boy."

"Do I? I wish other people thought so; but I tried for a place once, and the man looked at me as if he thought I'd start off early some mornin' with his cash-box, and declined engagin' me. Maybe he thought I looked too smart."

"Rufie wouldn't steal for anything!" said Rose, with indignant emphasis.

"I don't know about that. I've stolen you this mornin'. I expect Mr. Martin will open his eyes wider'n usual when he finds you are gone. I'll tell you what I'll do, Miss Manning," he continued, turning to the seamstress. "As near as I can make out, Rose will cost about three dollars a week."

"That's too much. Sixty-two cents and a dollar and a quarter make not quite two dollars."

"I know that, but you will want to live a little better than you have done. You must have meat oftener, and will want fire all the time when it's cold.

Then it won't do you any hurt to have a good cup **of** tea every night."

"But three dollars seem a good deal for you **to** pay," expostulated Miss Manning.

"Don't trouble yourself about that. I can work more cheerful, if I know that Rose is comfortable. Maybe, if I'll buy her a book, you'll teach her a little every day."

"I will, and with great pleasure."

"Then I'll bring the book along to-night."

"Oh, there's one thing more," said Rough and Ready, suddenly. "Don't you want to take another boarder?"

"Another boarder?"

"Yes, I'd like to come round, and take supper with you every night. Breakfast I'll get at the Lodgin' House, and dinner at a restaurant, but it would be pleasant to come round, and eat supper with you and Rose."

"It would be pleasant for us also," said Miss Manning.

"I guess that'll cost you a dollar a week more, so I'll pay you four dollars a week."

" I don't like to have you pay so much. I feel as if I were making money out of you."

" I'll take care you don't. You don't know what an appetite I've got. I'll come round at six every evening, or before ; only six can be the hour for supper."

" Very well, Rufus, but you must promise me one thing."

" What is it ? "

" That if you find it is too hard on you to pay so much money, you will let me know."

" All right. So it's all settled ? "

" Yes."

" Good ! " said the newsboy, with an air of satisfaction. " Now I must be goin' to business. I don't know exactly what time it is, as I left my gold watch lyin' on the sofy in Leonard Street."

" Oh, what a story, Rufie ! " said Rose. " He hasn't got any gold watch, Miss Manning, and we didn't have any sofy in Leonard Street."

" That's the way she's always exposin' me, Miss Manning," said the newsboy, laughing.

" Well, Rosy, good-by. It's time for the evenin'

papers to be out, and I must be on hand, as the other boys."

He kissed his little sister, and hurried downstairs. As he was making his way towards the offices of the evening papers, he felt great satisfaction in thinking of his unexpected good fortune in finding so desirable a home for his little sister. Hitherto he had felt a great deal of anxiety about her, during his necessary absence during the day, knowing only too well the character of his stepfather. He had known that there was danger of little Rose being abused in his frequent fits of intoxication, and more than once his heart was filled with apprehension, as he ascended the stairs to the cold and cheerless room in Leonard Street, which he had been forced to call home for the lack of a better.

But now there was a great change for the better. He knew that Miss Manning would be kind to little Rose, and would take good care of her, as well as provide her with pleasant company, while he was on the street selling papers. It was pleasant to him also to reflect that the arrangement would be an advantageous one for the seamstress. He had noticed her pale cheek, and he felt sure that it proceeded, not only from steady and confining work, but also from a lack of nourishing food. She would now be able to live better and more comfortable, and without exceeding the sum which she had hitherto been accustomed to expend. In the first place, she would have to pay thirty-eight cents less weekly for rent, and though this may seem a very small sum to the boys and girls who may read my story, it represented to the poor seamstress the proceeds of an entire day's work, beginning at early morning, and extending for fourteen hours. So, while Rough and Ready thought principally of his sister, it pleased him to feel that in benefiting her he was also benefiting the one who had agreed to take charge of her.

Then, as to himself, although he would pass his nights at the Lodging House, and eat breakfast there, once a day he would be at the little room in Franklin Street, and this would make him feel that he had some share in his sister's home.

He made his way to the offices of the evening papers, obtained a supply, and was soon busily en gaged in disposing of them. While he is thus en

gaged, we must go back to Leonard Street, which
the newsboy and his sister have left, **as** they hope,
forever

CHAPTER VI.

MARTIN'S AWAKENING.

JAMES MARTIN lay in a drunken stupor for about an hour after Rough and Ready and his sister left the room. Then he roused a little, and muttered " Rose."

But there was no answer.

" Rose," he repeated, not stirring from his recumbent position, " have you got anything to eat in the house?"

But the little girl whom he addressed was already in her new home on Franklin Street.

" Why don't you answer?" demanded he, angrily. " I'll give you a licking."

As this threat also elicited no response, he turned over and rose slowly.

" The gal isn't here," he said, after looking about him. " She's gone out with her scamp of a brother.

He's an obstinate young rascal. I'll give him a flogging some time."

Martin had often had the disposition to inflict punishment upon our hero, but there was a sturdy courage and firmness about Rough and Ready that promised a determined opposition. So he had escaped where a weaker and more timid boy would have suffered bad treatment.

Though Martin missed Rose he had no idea yet that she had left him for good, as the saying is. He supposed that she had gone out to stand by her brother when he was selling papers. He had often been drunk before, and probably expected to be often again. He felt no particular shame at disposing of the little girl's clothes for rum. He had somehow formed the idea that it was the newsboy's duty to support the family, and felt that he had no business to spend so much money on his sister's dress. He could not understand, therefore, why Rough and Ready should be so angry.

"Dressing up Rose like a princess!" he muttered. "We're too poor to spend money on good clothes I have to go about in rags, and why shouldn't she?'

Martin wore a suit which had done long and hard service. He wore a jacket of green cloth, frayed and dirty, while his other garments, originally black, were stained and patched. He wore no collar or necktie. On his head was a tall hat, which had already reached that outward condition when it is usually considered fit only to supply the place of a broken pane.

Such was the stepfather of the newsboy and his sister, and when to the description I add inflamed eyes, a red face, and swollen nose, I think my young readers will hardly wonder that the children had long lost all respect and attachment for him, if indeed they had ever felt any. When I think of the comfortable home he might have had, for he was a skilful workman and capable of earning good wages, I feel out of patience with him for preferring to lead a life so degraded and useless, doing harm both to himself and to others. But, in a great city like New York, there are many men who lead lives no better than James Martin, who, for the brief pleasure of the intoxicating cup, throw away their own happiness and welfare, and spoil the happiness of others. Think of this

picture, boy-reader, and resolve thus early that such **a**
description shall never apply to you!

Feeling hungry, Martin looked into the cupboard,
and discovered part of a loaf of bread. He was disappointed to find no cold meat, as he had hoped.

" This is pretty poor living," he muttered. " That
boy must pay me more money. He don't work hard
enough. How can he expect three people to live on
fifty cents a day?"

It did not seem to occur to Martin that he ought to
have contributed something himself to the support of
the family. So, while he was eating the bread, he continued to rail against our hero, and resolved to exact
from him in future sixty cents daily.

" He can pay it, — a smart boy like him," he muttered. " He's lazy, that's what's the matter. He's
got to turn over a new leaf."

Having eaten up the bread, and feeling still hungry, he explored the contents of his pocket-book. It
contained twenty-five cents, being half of the money
he had received from the old-clothes dealer for the
little girl's dress.

" That'll buy me a drink and a plate of meat," **he**

thought; "only there won't be any left. Money don't go far in these days."

But persons who get money as this was got, are not very apt to be disturbed much by economical thoughts. "Easy come, easy go," is an old adage and a true one. So Martin, reflecting that the newsboy was out earning money, of which he would receive the benefit, saw nothing to prevent his using the balance of the money to gratify the cravings of appetite.

He accordingly went to a neighboring saloon, where he soon invested his money, and then, thrusting his hands in his empty pockets, strolled listlessly about the streets. Passing through the City Hall Square, he saw Rough and Ready, at a little distance, selling his papers.

"Rose isn't with him," said Martin to himself. "Maybe she's gone home."

However, this was a point in which he felt very little interest. There was no particular object in addressing the newsboy on the subject, so he wandered on in a listless way wherever caprice led.

Strolling down Broadway, he turned into Dey

Street, though he had no definite object in so doing. All at once he felt a touch upon his shoulder.

" Well, Martin, how goes it? " said a stout, active-looking man, of much more respectable appearance than Martin himself.

" Hard luck l" said Martin.

" Well, you don't look very prosperous, that's a fact.   Where are you at work now? "

" Nowhere."

" Can't you find work? "

" No," said Martin.

The fact was that he had not tried, preferring to live on the earnings of his stepson.

" That's strange," said the new-comer.   " Carpenters are in demand.   There's a good deal of building going on in Brooklyn just now. I'll give you employment myself, if you'll come over to-morrow morning. I'm putting up three houses on Fourth Avenue, and want to hurry them through as soon as possible, as they are already let, and the parties want to move in Come, what do you say? "

" I didn't think of going to work just yet," said

Martin, reluctantly. " The fact is, I don't feel quite strong."

" Perhaps there's a reason for that," said the other, significantly.

" I don't feel well, and that's all about it."

" Perhaps you drink a little too often."

" I don't drink enough to hurt me. It's all that keeps me up."

" Well, that's your affair, not mine. Only, if you make up your mind to go to work, come over to-morrow morning to Brooklyn, and I'll have something for you to do."

To this Martin assented, and the builder, for such was his business, passed on. Martin had very little thought of accepting the proposal; but, as we shall see, circumstances soon brought it to his mind, and changed his determination.

It is not necessary to follow Martin in his afternoon wanderings. He took no more drink, for the simple reason that he was out of money, and his credit was not good; so when evening came he was comparatively free from the influence of his earlier potations. About six o'clock he went back to the room in Leonard Street. It was about that time that Rough and Ready usually went home to eat his supper, and, as he was still hungry, he proposed to eat supper with the children.

But when he opened the door of the room, he was surprised to find it empty. He expected to find Rose there, at all events, even if her brother had not yet returned home.

" Rose," he cried out, " where are you?"

There was no answer.

" If you're hiding anywhere, you'd better come out, or I'll give you something you don't like."

" This is strange," he said to himself when again there was no reply.

He went across the landing, and knocked at the door opposite.

A stout woman, with her sleeves rolled up, opened the door.

" Have you seen anything of my two children, Mrs. Flanagan?" asked Martin.

" I saw them this morning."

" I mean since morning."

" No; the boy took the little girl out about the

middle of the day, and I haven't seen either one of
'em since."

" They didn't say anything to you about going out,
did they? "

" Shure they didn't, and why should they? They
go out every day, for that matter."

" Well, it's time for them to be home now."

" They'll be comin' soon, it's likely; " and Mrs.
Flanagan closed her door, and went back to washing,
— for this was her business.

Martin returned to the lonely room, not altogether
satisfied with what he had learned. It was, as he
knew, quite unusual for Rose to be gone out all the
afternoon, or, at any rate, not to be back at this
hour. Besides, as he called to mind, she was not
with Rough and Ready when he saw him in the afternoon. Where, then, could she be?

It was from no particular affection for Rose that
Martin put to himself these queries. But it was
through Rose that he retained his hold upon Rufus
and his earnings. Besides, Rose, though only seven
years old, had been accustomed to get the supper,
and make tea at times when Martin had not money

enough to buy any beverage more stimulating. So, on the whole, he felt rather uncomfortable, and resolved to go out and find the newsboy, and learn from him where Rose was. He descended the stairs, therefore, and made his way to the sidewalk in front of the "Times" office, where Rough and Ready was usually to be found. But here he looked for him in vain. The fact was that our hero had sold off his papers, and a large number of them, with greater rapidity than usual, and was at this very moment sitting at Miss Manning's little tab e with Rose, eating a comfortable, though not very extravagant, supper.

Martin went back to Leonard Street, therefore, still with a vague hope that he might find the children at home. But he was destined to be disappointed. The room was as dark and cheerless and lonely as ever.

"What does it all mean?" thought Martin. "Has the young rascal given me the slip?"

He had been in the room only five minutes, when there was a knock at the door.

It proved to be the landlord's agent, who collected the rent.

" Your month's rent is due, Mr. Martin," he said.

" I haven't got any money."

" That answer won't do, ' said the man, shortly.

" You'll have to come again to-morrow, at any rate. My boy's got the money for the rent, and he isn't in now."

" You must be ready to-morrow, or move out."

" I guess it'll be move then, if the boy doesn't come back," muttered Martin. " One good thing, he can't escape me. I can catch him to-morrow morning when he's selling papers. Rent or no rent, I'll get one more night's rest in this room."

Although it was yet early he lay down, and did not rise till the morning light entered the room. Then, feeling the cravings of appetite, he got up, and went out in search of the newsboy.

" He won't find it quite so easy to get rid of me as he thinks for," muttered Martin, with a scowl.

CHAPTER VII.

THE NEWSBOY AND HIS STEPFATHER.

ROUGH AND READY passed the night at the Lodging
House, as he had previously determined. The bed
which he obtained there was considerably better than
the one he had usually rested upon in the room in
Leonard Street. He slept soundly, and only awoke
when the summons came to all the boys to get up.
As our hero lifted up his head, and saw the rows of
beds, with boys sitting up and rubbing their eyes,
the thought of his freedom from the sway of his stepfather recurred to his mind, and he jumped up in
very good spirits. He breakfasted at the Lodge,
paying only six cents for the meal, and then hastened
to the offices of the morning papers to secure a supply of merchandise.

He began to estimate his probable weekly ex
penses. He had agreed to pay Miss Manning four
dollars a week for Rose's board and his own supper.

His expenses at the Lodging House would be seventy-two cents a week. His dinner would perhaps amount to a dollar more. This would be five dollars and seventy-two cents, which he must earn at any rate. But, besides this, both Rose and himself would need clothes. Probably these would cost annually fifty dollars apiece, averaging, for the two, two dollars per week. Thus his entire expenses footed up seven dollars and seventy-two cents, or about one dollar and twenty-nine cents per working day.

"That is considerable," thought the newsboy. "I wonder if I can do it."

Some boys might have been frightened at this estimate. But Rough and Ready had good courage. He felt that his sister and he could not live comfortably for less, and he resolved that if he could not make it all by selling papers, he would get a chance to do errands, or manage in some other way to eke out the necessary amount. But he resolved to make his newspaper trade pay as much of it as possible. He went to work, therefore, with a good deal of energy, and the pile of morning papers, with which he started, melted away fast. At last he had but one left. Looking out for a purchaser for that, he saw advancing towards him an old woman, dressed in quaint, old-fashioned costume.

"Won't you let me look at that paper of yourn?" asked the old lady.

"Certainly, ma'am," said Rough and Ready; "it's made to be looked at."

"Wait a minute. I dunno as I've got my specs," said she, diving her hand into a pocket of great depth, and bringing up first a snuff-box, and next a red cotton handkerchief.

"There, I know'd I'd mislaid 'em," she said, in a tone of disappointment. "Can you read, boy?"

"More or less," said Rough and Ready. "What is it you wanted?"

"Why, you see I live to Danbury when I'm at home, and I heerd tell that Roxanna Jane Pinkham was married, and I want to know ef it's true. Maybe you'll find it in the marriages."

"All right, ma'am," said Rough and Ready, glancing over the paper till he came to the list of marriages.

"Is this it, ma'am?" asked the newsboy, reading,

"In Danbury, Miss Roxanna Jane Pinkham to Pompey Smith, a very respectable colored man from New York."

"Massy sakes!" ejaculated the old lady. "Has Roxanna married a nigger? Well, she must have been put to't for a husband. Thank you, boy. I'd buy your paper, but I only wanted to know for certain if Roxanna was married. That does beat me, — her marryin' a colored person!"

"That's a profitable customer," thought the newsboy. "I guess she won't find that marriage in any of the other papers. This one has got it exclusive."

Immediately upon her return, the old lady spread the news of Roxanna Pinkham's strange marriage, and wrote comments upon it to her daughter in Danbury. When the report was indignantly denied by the lady most interested, and she threatened to sue the old lady for circulating a slanderous report, the latter stoutly asserted that she heard it read from a New York paper, and she had no doubt there was something in it, or it wouldn't have got into print.

This trick was hardly justifiable in the newsboy; but he was often troubled by people who wanted to

6

look at his papers, but were not willing to buy them, and he repaid himself by some imaginary news of a startling description.

After disposing of his last paper, he procured a fresh supply, and was engaged in selling these, when, on looking up, he saw advancing towards him James Martin, his stepfather.

Before chronicling the incidents of the interview between them, we must go back to the time of Martin's awaking in the room in Leonard Street.

He remembered, at once, the visit of the landlord's agent the day previous, and felt that the time for action had arrived. He knew that the scanty furniture in the room was liable to seizure for rent, and this he resolved the landlord should not get hold of. Accordingly, dressing hastily, he went round to Baxter Street, and accosted the proprietor of a general second-hand establishment, with whom he had previously had some dealings.

" I've got some furniture to sell," he said. " Do you want to buy?"

" I don't know," said the other. " Trade is very dull. I don't sell a dollar's worth in a day."

" Come, you shall have them cheap," said Martin.

" What have you got?"

" Come and see."

" Where is it?"

" In Leonard Street, just round the corner."

The dealer, always ready for a bargain, was induced to climb up to the attic room, and take a look at the cheap wooden bedstead, with its scanty bedding, and the two chairs, which were about all the furniture the room contained.

" It's not worth much," he said.

" Well, I suppose it's worth something," said Martin.

" What'll you take for it?"

" Three dollars."

" I'll give you one dollar."

" That's too bad. You ought to give me two dollars, at any rate."

At length, after considerable chaffering, the dealer agreed to give a dollar and a quarter, which Martin pocketed with satisfaction.

Just as he had effected the sale, the landlord's agent appeared.

" Have you got your rent ready?" he asked of Martin.

" No, I haven't," said Martin.

" Then you must move out."

" I'm just moving."

" But I shall seize the furniture," said the agent. " I can't allow you to move that."

" Take it, if you want to," said Martin, in a coarse laugh " I've just sold it to this man here."

" I don't believe it," said the agent, angrily.

" Oh, well, it's nothing to me. Settle it between you," said Martin, carelessly, going downstairs, leaving the dealer and the agent to an animated and angry dispute over the broken-down bedstead.

" That was neatly done," thought Martin, laughing to himself. " I don't care which gets it. I suppose they'll have a fight about it. Now I must have a good breakfast, and then for a talk with that young rebel. He thinks he's cheated me cleverly, but I'm not through with him yet."

Martin strayed into a restaurant at the lower end of Chatham Street, where he made a satisfactory breakfast, with as little regard to expense as if his resources were ample. Indeed, he felt little trouble about the future, being fully determined that in the future, as in the past, Rufus should support him.

"Aint I entitled to his earnings, I'd like to know till he comes of age?" thought Martin.

So he convinced himself readily that law and right were on his side, and it was with no misgivings as to the result that he approached the newsboy whom, from some distance away, he saw actively engaged in plying his business.

"'Herald,' 'Tribune,' 'Times,' 'World'!" cried Rough and Ready, looking about him for possible customers.

"So I've found you at last," said James Martin, grimly addressing the newsboy.

"I haven't been lost that I know of," said Rough and Ready, coolly.

"Where were you last night?"

"At the Newsboys' Lodge."

"What made you leave home?"

"I didn't like staying there."

"You're a mighty independent young man. How old do you pretend to be?"

" Fifteen, as near as I can remember," said the newsboy.

" I didn't know but you were twenty-one, as you claim to be your own master," sneered Martin.

" I don't see why I shouldn't be my own master,' said Rough and Ready, " as long as I have to support myself."

" Aint I your father?"

" No, you aint," said the newsboy, bitterly. " You married my mother, and killed her with your ill-treatment. I don't want to have anything more to do with you."

" Oh, you're mighty smart. What have you done with your sister?"

" She's safe," said the newsboy, shortly.

" What business had you to take her away from her home?" demanded Martin, angrily.

" I've got the care of her."

" She's my child, and you must bring her back again."

" Your child!" said Rufus, contemptuously. " You did not give a cent towards supporting her. What little you earned you spent for rum. I had to pay all the expenses, and when I bought my sister some new clothes, you were mean enough to carry them off and sell them. If it hadn't been for that, I would have left her a little while longer. But that was more than I could stand, and I've carried her where you won't find her."

"Tell me, instantly, where you have carried her," said James Martin, stung by the newsboy's reproaches, and doggedly resolved to get the little girl back, at all hazards.

"I don't mean to tell you," said Rough and Ready.

"Why not?"

"Because she is in a good place, where she will be taken care of, and I don't mean that you shall get hold of her again."

"You'd better take care what you say," said Martin, his red nose growing redder still, in his angry excitement.

"I'm not afraid of your threats," said the newsboy, quietly.

"I've a great mind to give you a flogging on the spot."

"I wouldn't advise you to try it, unless you want me to call a copp."

James Martin had no great love for the police, with whom he had before now got into difficulty. Besides, he knew that Rufus, though not as strong as himself, was strong enough to make a very troublesome resistance to any violence, and that the disturbance would inevitably attract the attention of the police. So he forbore to attack him, though he found it hard to resist the impulse. But he shook his fist menacingly at Rufus, and said, "Some day I'll get hold of your sister, you may be sure of that, and when I do, I'll put her where you'll never set eyes on her again. Just remember that!"

He went off muttering, leaving Rufus a little troubled. He knew that his stepfather had an ugly spirit, and he feared that he would keep on the watch for Rose, and some day might get hold of her. The very thought was enough to make him tremble. He determined to warn Miss Manning of the danger which threatened his little sister, and request her to be very careful of her, keeping her continually under her eye.

CHAPTER VIII.

ROSE IN HER NEW HOME.

AT the close of the afternoon the newsboy, count-ing up his gains, found that he had made a dollar and a half by selling papers, and twenty-five cents besides, by an errand which he had done for a shop-keeper whose boy was sick. If he could keep up this rate of wages every day, he would be able to get along very well. But, in the first place, it was not often that he made as much as a dollar and a half by selling papers, nor was there a chance to do errands every day. When it was rainy his sales of papers fell off, as there were not so many people about Rufus began to feel like a family man, with the re sponsibility of supporting a family on his hands.

He was determined that his little sister should not be obliged to go out into the street to earn anything, though there are many girls, no older than she, who are sent out with matches, or papers, or perhaps to beg. But Rufus was too proud to permit that.

"A stout boy like me ought to earn money enough to take care of two persons," he said to himself.

About half-past five he started for Franklin Street, for it will be remembered that he had arranged to take supper with his sister and Miss Manning.

Rose had been listening for his step, and as soon as she heard it on the stairs, she ran out on the landing, and called out, joyfully, "Is that you, Rufie?"

"Yes, Rosie," said the newsboy. "What have you been doing to-day?"

"I've had such a nice time, Rufie," said the little girl, clinging to her brother's arm. "Miss Manning began to teach me my letters to-day."

"How does she get along, Miss Manning?" asked Rough and Ready, who by this time had entered the room.

"Famously," said Miss Manning. "She's very quick. I think she'll be able to read in three months, if she keeps on doing as well as to-day."

"That's good," said the newsboy, with satisfaction. "I've always been afraid that she would grow up ignorant, and I shouldn't like that."

"I'm no great scholar," said Miss Manning, modestly; "but I shall be glad to teach Rose all I can."

"I am afraid it will be a good deal of trouble for you."

"No, it is very little. Rose sits beside me, learning, while I am sewing."

"But you have to leave off to hear her."

"Leaving off now and then rests me. Besides, as you pay part of my rent, I do not need to work so steadily as I used to do."

"I've a great mind to ask you to teach me a little, too, Miss Manning," said the newsboy.

"I'll do it with pleasure, as far as I am capable. How much do you know?"

"Precious little," said Rufus. "I can read some, but when I get out of easy reading I can't do much."

"Can you write?"

"A little, but not much."

"I will help you all I can."

"Then I'll bring a writing book to-morrow evening, and a book to read out of."

Rough and Ready, though not as ignorant as many in his situation in life, had long deplored his ignorance, and wished that he knew more. But he had been obliged to work early and late, and his stepfather was not one to give him assistance, or take any interest in his improvement. So he had grown up ignorant, though possessed of excellent abilities, because he saw no way of obtaining the knowledge he desired. Now, however, he thought, with Miss Manning's help, he might enter upon a career of improvement.

"Have you seen father yet, Rufie?" asked Rose, uneasily.

"I saw Mr. Martin this morning," said the newsboy, emphasizing the name, for he would not recognize any relationship between them.

"I mean Mr. Martin," said Rose. "What did he say?"

"He wanted to know where you were."

"Did he?" asked Rose, looking frightened.

"Don't be afraid, Rosie," said her brother, putting his arm round his little sister's neck. "He doesn't know, and I shan't let him find out."

"But if he should find out," said Rose, in terror. "You won't let him carry me off."

"No, I won't. Don't be frightened. Do you like this better than Leonard Street, Rosie?"

"Oh, ever so much."

Rufus looked pleased. He felt that he had made the best arrangement in his power for his sister's comfort and happiness, and that he had been very lucky to find so suitable a person as Miss Manning to place her with.

While he was talking with Rose, the seamstress had been moving about quietly, and by this time the little table was neatly spread in the centre of the room. On it were placed knives, forks, and plates for three. The teakettle had boiled, and, taking out her little teapot, the seamstress put it on the stove for the tea to steep.

"Do you like toast, Rufus?" she asked.

"Yes, Miss Manning; but I don't want you to take too much trouble."

"It's very little trouble. I think Rose would like toast too. I've got a little meat too."

She took from the cupboard about half a pound of steak, which she put on the coals to broil.

"I'm afraid you're giving us too good a supper," said the newsboy. "Beefsteak costs considerable. I don't want you to lose money by Rose and me."

"There is no danger of that," said Miss Manning. "It doesn't cost as much as you think for. The steak only cost me twelve cents."

"But there's the tea and the toast," suggested Rough and Ready.

"Toast costs no more than bread, and six cents pays for all the bread we eat at night. Then I only need a spoonful or two of tea, and that, and the sugar and butter altogether, don't cost more than eighteen cents."

"Do you mean that we can live like this for thirty cents a meal?" asked the newsboy, incredulously. "Why, I have about as much as that to pay for my dinner at the eating-house, and the meat isn't as good as this, I am sure."

"Yes, they charge considerable for the cooking and the profits," said Miss Manning. "I do the cooking myself, and save all that."

By this time dinner, as we may call it, was ready, and the three sat down to the table.

It was, to be sure, an humble meal; but it looked very attractive and inviting for all that, with the steak on a plate in the centre, the well-browned toast on one side, and the little plate of butter on the other, while the little teapot steamed with its fra· grant beverage. It was so different from the way in which they had lived in Leonard Street, that it seemed very pleasant to the two children.

" Isn't it nice, Rufie?" said Rose.

" Yes," said the newsboy. " It's what I call reg-'larly jolly. Besides, it cost so little money, I can't get over that. I'm sure we're much obliged to Miss Manning."

" But," said the seamstress, " you must remember that if it's better for you, it's better and pleasanter for me too. You mustn't think I used to live like this before Rose came to me. I couldn't afford to. Sometimes I had a little tea, but not often, and it was very seldom that I ate any meat. The rent came hard for me to pay, and I had to work so steadily

that I didn't feel as if I could afford time to cook anything, even if I had the money to buy it with."

" What did you have for supper, Miss Manning?"
inquired Rose.

" Generally I didn't get anything but dry bread,
without butter or tea."

" But I should think you would have felt hungry
for something else."

" I didn't have much appetite. I sat so steadily
at my work, without a chance to breathe the fresh
air, that I cared very little about eating. My appetite is beginning to come now."

" I think you and Rose had better take a walk
every day," said Rufus. " You both need to breathe
the fresh air. That is, if you think you can spare
the time."

" Oh, yes, I can spare the time, now that I get paid
so well for my boarder," said the seamstress, playfully. " An hour or two of my time is worth very
little. How much do you think I earn when I sit
over my work all day, — about fourteen hours?"

" I don't know," said Rufus. " I think you ought
to earn as much as a dollar."

Miss Manning shook her head, with a smile.

"I see you know very little about the wages paid to us poor seamstresses," she said. "If I were paid a dollar for my day's work I should feel as if I were worth a fortune."

"But you earn near that," said the newsboy, "don't you?"

"When I work steadily, I earn about three shillings," said Miss Manning.

I must here remind my New England reader, who is accustomed to consider a shilling about seventeen cents, that in New York eight shillings are reckoned to the dollar, and a shilling, therefore, only repre sents twelve and a half cents; Miss Manning's day's work thus brought her thirty-seven and a half cents.

"Three shillings!" repeated Rough and Ready, in surprise. "That's very poor pay. I think I do very poorly if I don't make as much as a dollar. Won't they pay you any more?"

"No, they find plenty who are ready to take their work at the price they are willing to pay. If anybody complains, they take away their work and employ somebody else."

"How much do you think I made to day?" asked
the newsboy

"A dollar and a quarter?"

"I made a dollar and seventy-five cents," said
Rough and Ready, with satisfaction.

"Rufie's real smart," said Rose, who was proud
of her brother, in whom she felt implicit confidence.

"You mustn't believe all she says, Miss Manning," said the newsboy, laughing. "Rose thinks
more of me than anybody else does. But what were
we talking about? Oh, about going out for a walk
every day. If you think you can spare the time to
go out with Rose, I think it will do you both good."

"We can come round and see you sell papers sometimes, Rufie," said his little sister.

"No," said the newsboy, hastily, "I don't want
you to do that."

"Why not?" said Rose, surprised.

"Because Mr. Martin is on the lookout for Rose,
and will very likely be prowling round somewhere
near me, ready to pounce on Rose if he happens to
see her. So I'd rather you'd keep on the west side
with her, Miss Manning. If you go on Broadway,

let it be somewhere above Chamber Street, where you won't be seen from the Park. In that way Martin won't be likely to meet you."

"It is best to be prudent, no doubt," said Miss Manning. "I will remember your wishes."

The next evening, Rufus began to study, under the guidance and direction of Miss Manning. He generally left the room about nine o'clock, and made his way to the Newsboys' Lodge, where he now passed his nights regularly.

CHAPTER IX.

MR. MARTIN'S PECUNIARY TROUBLES.

James Martin, after his unsatisfactory interview with Rough and Ready, found it necessary to make some plans for the future. He had been forced to leave the rooms in Leonard Street; he had no longer the newsboy's earnings to depend upon, and, disagreeable as it was to work for his own living, there really seemed no other way open to him. On the whole, as he had no home and no money, he was not particular about resuming the care of Rose at once.

He was willing that her brother should retain the charge of her at present at his own expense, but none the less was he angry with Rough and Ready for defying his authority.

"I'll get hold of the girl yet, in spite of him," he said to himself. "He'll find out what I am before I get through with him."

In the mean time, he thought of the work which had

been offered him in Brooklyn, and resolved, as a matter of necessity, to go over and see if he could not effect an engagement. The new houses he remembered were on Fourth Avenue, in Brooklyn He did not know exactly where, but presumed he could find out.

He crossed Fulton Ferry, luckily having two cents about him. Fourth Avenue is situated in that part of Brooklyn which is known as Gowanus, and is at least two miles from the ferry. The fare by the horse-cars was six cents, but James Martin had only three left after paying his ferriage. He could not make up his mind to walk, however, and got into the Greenwood cars, resolved to trust his luck. The cars started, and presently the conductor came round.

Martin put his hand into his pocket unconcernedly, and, starting in apparent surprise, felt in the other.

"Some rascal must have picked my pocket," he said. "My pocket-book is gone."

"How much money did you have in it?" asked his next neighbor.

"Forty-five dollars and twenty-five cents," said

Martin, with unblushing falsehood. "It's pretty hard on a poor man."

The conductor looked rather incredulous, observing his passenger's red nose, and that his breath was mingled with fumes of whiskey.

"I'm sorry for you if you've lost your pocket-book," he said; "but can't you raise six cents?"

Martin again thrust his hand into his pocket, and drew out three cents.

"That's all I've got left," he said. "You'll have to take me for half price."

"Contrary to orders," said the conductor. "Couldn't do it."

"What am I to do then?"

"If you can't pay your fare, you'll have **to get off** the cars."

"It seems to me you're rather hard," said a passenger.

"I have to obey orders," said the conductor. "I don't make the regulations myself."

"If you will allow me," said a lady opposite, "I will pay your fare, sir."

"Thank you, ma'am," said Martin. "I'll accept

your kind offer, though I wouldn't need to be be-holden to anybody, if it hadn't been for my loss. It's pretty hard on a poor man," he added, com-plainingly.

"Will you accept a trifle towards making up your loss?" said an old gentleman, who had more benevo-lence than penetration.

"Thank you, sir," said James Martin, accepting the two-dollar bill which was tendered him, without feeling the least delicacy in so doing.

"You're very kind. I wouldn't take it if I hadn't been so unfortunate."

"You're quite welcome," said the old gentleman, kindly. "You'd better report your loss to the police."

"So I shall, as soon as I return to-night."

James Martin looked round among the other pas-sengers, hoping that some one else might be induced to follow the example of the charitable old gentle man. But he was disappointed. There was some thing about his appearance, which was not exactly engaging or attractive, and his red nose inspired sus-picions that his habits were not quite what they ought to have been. In fact, there was more than one passenger who had serious doubts as to the reality of his loss.

When the cars reached the entrance of Fourth Avenue, Martin descended, and walked up the street.

" Well, ' he said, chuckling, as he drew out the bill from his pocket, " I'm in luck. I'd like to meet plenty as soft-headed as that old chap that gave it to me. He swallowed down my story, as if it was gospel. I'll try it again some time when I'm hard up."

Martin began to consider whether, having so large a sum on hand, he had not better give up the idea of working till the next day ; but the desire to find himself in a position in which he could regain Rose prevailed over his sluggishness, and he decided to keep on.

He had not far to walk. He soon came in sight of a row of wooden houses which were being erected, and, looking about him, he saw the man he .had met in the streets of New York only a day or two before.

" Hallo, Martin ! " he called out, seeing the new arrival ; " have you come over to help us?"

"Do you need any help?" asked Martin.

"Badly. One of my men is sick, and I am short-handed."

"What do you give?"

"Two dollars a day."

Wages are higher now, but this was before the war.

"Come, what do you say?"

"Well, I might as well," said Martin.

"Then I'll tell you what I would like to have you begin on."

The directions were given, and James Martin set to work. He was in reality an excellent workman, and the only thing which had reduced him to his present low fortune was the intemperate habits which had for years been growing upon him. Mr. Blake, the contractor, himself a master carpenter, understood this, and was willing to engage him, because he knew that his work would be done well as long as he was in a fit condition to work.

Martin kept at work till six o'clock, when all the workmen knocked off work. He alone had no boarding place to go to.

" Where do you board, Tarbox?" he asked of a
fellow-workman.

" In Eighth Street," he answered.

" Is it a good place? "

" Fair."

" Who keeps the house?"

" Mrs. Waters."

" What do you pay?"

" Four dollars a week."

This again was lower than the price which mechanics have to pay now.

" Is there room for another?"

" Yes, the old lady'll be glad to get another.   Will
you come?"

" Well, I'll try it."

So James Martin walked home with Tarbox, and was
introduced to Mrs. Waters, — a widow who looked
as if it required hard work and anxious thought to
keep her head above water.   Of course she was glad
to get another boarder, and her necessities were such
that she could not afford to be particular, or possibly
Mr. Martin's appearance might have been an objection.

" I suppose," she said, " you won't have any objection to go in with Mr. Tarbox."

" No," said Martin, " not at present; but I may be bringing my little girl over here before long. Do you think you can find room for her?"

" She might sleep with my little girl," said Mrs. Waters; " that is, if you don't object. How old is she?"

" She is seven."

" And my Fanny is eight. They'd be company for each other."

" My little girl is in New York, at present," said Mr. Martin, " stopping with — with a relative. I shall leave her there for a while."

" You can bring her any time, Mr. Martin," said Mrs. Waters. " If you will excuse me now, I will go and see about the supper."

In ten minutes the bell rang, and the boarders went down to the basement to eat their supper.

Considering Mrs. Waters' rate of board, which has already been mentioned, it will hardly be expected that her boarding establishment was a very stylish one. Indeed, style would hardly have been appreciated by the class of boarders which patronized her A table, covered with a partially dirty cloth, stood in the centre of the room. On this were laid out plates and crockery of common sort, and a good supply of plain food, including cold meat. Mrs. Waters found that her boarders were more particular about quan tity than quality, and the hearty appetite which they brought with them after a day's work in the open air caused them to make serious inroads even upon the most bountiful meal which she could spread before them.

James Martin surveyed the prospect with satisfac- tion. He had lived in a slip-shod manner for some months, and the table set by Mrs. Waters, humble as it was, seemed particularly attractive. On the whole, he could not help feeling that it was better than Leonard Street. Indeed, he felt in particularly good spirits. He had two dollars in his pocket, and had worked three quarters of a day, thus earning a dol- lar and a half, though he would not be paid for his labor till the end of the week. The thought did come to him once, that after all he was well rid of Rose, as she would be an expense to him, and this expense the newsboy had voluntarily assumed. Now he had only himself to take care of. Why should he not give up the thought of reclaiming her?"

But then, on the other hand, Rough and Ready's independent course had offended him, and he felt a desire to "come up" with him. He knew that nothing would strike the newsboy a severer blow than to deprive him of his sister, and leave him in uncertainty as to her fate. Revenge he felt would be sweet, and he fully determined that he would have revenge.

"Let him look out for himself!" said James Martin. "I'll plague him yet. He'll be sorry for his cursed impudence, or my name isn't James Martin."

After supper Martin strolled out, and was not long in finding a liquor-shop. Here he supplied himself with a vile draught, that had the effect of making his red nose yet redder when he appeared at the breakfast-table the next morning. However, he didn't drink to excess, and was able to resume work the following day.

We must now leave him, awhile, and turn to little Rose and her brother.

CHAPTER X.

WHAT THE NEWSBOY FOUND.

It has been already stated that Rough and Ready had made a careful estimate of his expenses, and found that to meet them, including clothing, he must average seven dollars and seventy-two cents weekly. He might get along on less, but he was ambitious of maintaining himself and his sister in comfort.

This was a considerable sum for a newsboy to earn, and most boys in our hero's position would have felt discouraged. But Rough and Ready had an uncommon degree of energy and persistence, and he resolutely determined that in some way the weekly sum should be obtained. In some honest way, of course, for our hero, though not free from faults, was strictly honest, and had never knowingly appropriated a cent that did not justly belong to him. But he was not averse to any method by which he might earn an honest penny.

During the first fortnight after Rose came under the charge of Miss Manning, the newsboy earned fifteen dollars. His expenses during that time, including the amount paid for his sister, amounted to ten dollars and a half. This left four dollars and a half clear. This sum Rufus put into a savings-bank, knowing that after a time it would be necessary to purchase clothing both for himself and his sister, and for this purpose a reserve fund would be required.

One day, after selling his supply of morning papers, he wandered down to the Battery. This, as some of my readers may need to be informed, is a small park situated at the extreme point of Manhattan Island. It was on a delightful promenade, covered with grass, and shaded by lofty sycamore-trees. Around it formerly lived some of the oldest and most aristocratic families in the city. But its ancient glory, its verdure and beauty, have departed, and it is now unsightly and neglected. None of its old attractions remain, except the fine view which it affords of the bay, the islands, and fortifications, and the opposite shores of New Jersey. The old families have moved far up-town, and the neighborhood is given to sailors' boarding-houses, warehouses, **and** fourth-rate hotels and bar-rooms.

The newsboy strayed into one of these bar-rooms, not with any idea of drinking, for he never had been tempted to drink. The example of his stepfather had been sufficient to disgust him with intemperance. But it was an idle impulse that led him to enter. He sat down in a chair, and took up a copy of the " Morning Herald," of which he had sold a considerable number of copies, without having had a chance to read it.

Chancing to cast his eyes on the floor, he saw a pocket-book. He stooped down and picked it up, and slipped it into his pocket. He looked about him to see if there was any one present that was likely to have lost it. But, besides the bar-keeper, there was no one in the room except a rough-looking laborer in his shirt-sleeves, and it was evident that it did not belong to him, as he drew from his vest-pocket the money with which he paid for his potation.

The newsboy concluded that the pocket-book be-longed to some patron of the bar, who had dropped it, and gone away without missing it. The question came up, what should he do with it? Was it his duty to hand it to the bar-keeper?

He decided that it was not. Bar-keepers are apt to have easy consciences, and this one was not a very attractive representative of his class. He would undoubtedly pocket the wallet and its contents, and the true owner, if he should ever turn up, would stand very little chance of recovering his money.

These reflections quickly passed through the mind of our hero, and he decided to retain the pocket-book, and consult some one, in whom he reposed confidence, as to the proper course to pursue. He had no idea how much the wallet contained, and did not venture to examine it while he remained where he was. He decided to ask Mr. O'Connor, the superintendent of the Lodging House, what he had better do under the circumstances.

" I will remain here awhile," thought Rough and Ready. " Maybe the owner of the wallet will miss it, and come back for it. If he does, and I am sure it is his, I will give it up. But I won't give it to the bar-keeper ; I don't like his looks."

So Rufus remained in his seat reading the "Herald." He had never read the paper so faithfully before. While he was still reading, a sailor staggered in. He had evidently been drinking before, and showed the effects of it.

"A glass of rum," he said, in a thick voice.

"All right, sir," said the bar-keeper, obsequiously.

"I'm bound to have a jolly time," said the sailor. "I've just come back from a voyage, and I mean to make the money fly while I have it."

So saying, he drew out half-a-dozen bank-bills, rolled up tightly together.

"That's the talk," said the bar-keeper, complaisantly. "Nothing like being jolly."

"I say, you drink with me," said the sailor. "I don't want to drink alone."

"Certainly, thank you;" and the bar-keeper poured out a glass for himself.

"Isn't there anybody that would like a drink?" said the sailor.

He looked around him, and his glance fell on Rough and Ready.

"Won't that boy drink?" he asked.

" You had better ask him."

" I say, won't you have a drink?" said the sailor, turning to the newsboy.

" No, I thank you," said the newsboy.

" Are you too proud to drink with a rough fellow like me?"

" No," said our hero; " but I never drink. I don't like it."

" Well, my lad, I don't know but you're right," said the sailor, more soberly. " My mother asked me not to drink; but I couldn't hold out. Don't do it, if you don't like it."

The bar-keeper by this time thought fit to interfere.

" Look here, boy," he said, angrily, " we don't want any temperance lectures here. You've stayed as long as you're wanted. You needn't come in here hurting our trade."

Rough and Ready did not think it necessary to answer this tirade, but laid down the paper and went out, carrying the pocket-book with him, of course. He did not open it, even after he got into the street, for the action would be noticed, and it might excite suspicion if he were seen counting over a roll of bills,

which he judged from the feeling the wallet coi
tained.

It was now time to lay in his supply of afternoon
papers, and he therefore turned his steps to the offices, and was soon busily engaged in disposing of
them. Indeed, so busily was he occupied, that he
quite forgot he had the wallet in his possession.
The papers sold readily, and it was not till he was
ready to go to supper with Miss Manning and Rose
that the thought of his discovery returned to him.

" I will wait and open the pocket-book when I get
to the room," he said to himself.

" Well, Rose," he said, gayly, on entering the
room, " what do you think I've found?"

" I wish it was a kitten," said Rose.

" No, it isn't that," said Rufus, laughing, " and I
don't think I should take the trouble to pick it up, if
I did find one."

" Do you like kittens, Rose?" asked Miss Manning.

" Yes, very much," said Rose ; " they are so pretty
and playful."

" Would you like to have me get one for you?"

" Will you?" asked the child, eagerly.

" Yes ; there's a lodger on the lower floor has three. No doubt she will give us one."

" But won't it trouble you, Miss Manning?" asked the newsboy. " If it will, don't get it. Rose can get along without it."

" Oh, I like kittens myself," said Miss Manning ; " I should really like one."

" Now I like dogs best," said Rough and Ready.

" Most boys do, I believe," said the seamstress.

" But kittens are much prettier, Rufie," said Rose.

" They'll scratch, and dogs won't," said the newsboy ; " but if you like a kitten, and Miss Manning is kind enough to get you one, I shall be glad to have her do so. But you seem to have forgotten all about my discovery."

" What is it, Rufie?"

Rough and Ready drew the pocket-book from his pocket, and displayed it.

" Where did you find it, Rufus?" asked Miss Manning.

" Is there much money in it, Rufie?" asked his sister.

"I don't know yet, I'll look and see, and after-wards I'll tell where I found it."

He opened the wallet, and drew out a roll of bills. Spreading them open, he began to count. To his surprise they proved to be bills of a large denomination. There was one one-hundred-dollar bill, five twenties, six tens, and eight fives. He raised his eyes in surprise.

"Why, here are three hundred dollars," he said.

"Three hundred dollars!" exclaimed Rose, clapping her hands. "Why Rufie, how rich you are!"

"But it isn't my money, Rose," he said. "You must remember that. I may find the owner."

"Oh, I hope you won't," said the little girl, looking disappointed.

"But it isn't right to wish that, Rose," said Miss Manning. "Suppose you had lost the money, you would like to have it returned to you, would you not?"

"I suppose I should," said Rose; "but three hundred dollars would do us a great deal of good. You and Rufie wouldn't have to work so hard."

"As for me, hard work won't hurt me," said the

newsboy. " I rather enjoy it, now that I don't have to give my wages to Mr. Martin to buy rum with."

" Have you seen him lately? "

" Not since the time I mentioned. But now I will tell you where I found this money."

Hereupon the newsboy gave the account which is already known to the reader. It will, of course, be unnecessary to repeat it here. When he had finished speaking, Miss Manning asked, " Well, Rufus, what do you intend to do about the money? "

" I am going to ask Mr. O'Connor's advice about it to-night," said our hero. " Whatever he says I ought to do, I will do."

" Perhaps you won't find any owner, Rufie."

" We won't count our eggs before they are hatched," said Rufus, " and speaking of eggs, when are you going to give us some more for supper, Miss Manning? Those we had Monday were bully."

" We'll have them often, if you like them, Rufus," said the seamstress.

In five minutes they sat down to supper, in which, as usual, Rufus did full justice.

CHAPTER XI.

THE ADVERTISEMENT IN THE HERALD.

ABOUT eight o'clock Rough and Ready bade good-night to Miss Manning and his sister, and went round to the Newsboys' Lodge to sleep.

On entering the room he went up to the superintendent, and said, " Mr. O'Connor, I want to ask your advice about something."

" Very well, Rufus, I will give you the best advice in my power. Now what is it?"

Hereupon the newsboy told the story of his finding the pocket-book.

" Didn't you see any one to whom you think it was likely to belong?"

"No, sir."

" How long did you remain after you found it?"

"I waited about half an hour, thinking that the loser might come back for it; but no one came."

" Why did you not give it to the bar-keeper?"

" Because I knew it did not belong to him, and I judged from his looks that, if he once got hold of it, the true owner would never see it again, even if he came back for it."

" I have no doubt you are right. I only asked to learn your own idea about it. Now, what do you think of doing?"

" Wouldn't it be a good plan to advertise it in the 'Herald'?"

"Yes, I think it might. Besides, there is the chance of its loss being advertised there, so that we can examine the advertisements of articles lost."

" Yes, sir; will you write an advertisement?"

" If you wish me to do so."

The superintendent took pen and paper, and drew up the following advertisement:—

"FOUND. — A pocket-book, containing a considerable sum of money. The owner can have the same by calling on the Superintendent of the Newsboys' Lodging House, proving property, and paying the expense of this advertisement."

" How will that do?" he inquired.

"It's just the thing," said Rough and Ready "How many times shall I put it in?"

"Three times will answer, I think. I will give you enough of the money to pay for the advertise. ment, and you can carry it round to-night."

This was done. The charge was found to be fouɪ dollars and eighty cents, as the "Herald" charges forty cents per line, and the three insertions made twelve lines.

"I have no doubt," said Mr. O'Connor, "I shall have some applications from adventurers, who will pretend that they have lost a pocket-book ; but I will take care that it shall be surrendered only to the real owner."

The superintendent was right in this matter Early the next morning, a flashily attired individual mounted the long flights of stairs, and inquired foɪ him.

"What is your business, sir?" inquired Mr O'Connor.

"I called about that pocket-book which you adver· tise in the 'Herald.' "

"Have you lost one?"

" Yes, and I have no doubt that is the one. How much did you pay for advertising? I don't mind giving you a trifle extra for your trouble."

" Wait a moment. Where did you lose your pocket-book?"

" Really I can't say. I was at a good many places down town."

" Then you couldn't give any idea as to where you lost it?"

"I think I must have dropped it somewhere in Nassau Street or Fulton Street. Where was it found?"

" I do not intend giving information, but to require it. It is important that I should not give it to the wrong party."

" Do you doubt that the pocket-book is mine?" said the other, in an offended tone.

" I know nothing about it. If it is yours you can describe the pocket-book, and tell me how much money there is in it."

" Well," said the flashy individual, hesitating, " it wasn't a very large pocket-book."

" Brown?"

" Yes."

"And how much money was there in it?"

"Really, I couldn't tell exactly."

"But you can give me some idea?"

"There was somewhere from fifty to seventy-five dollars," said the adventurer, hazarding a guess.

"Then it doesn't belong to you," said the superintendent.

"There might have been a little more. Now I think of it, there must have been over eighty dollars."

"You are wasting your time, sir; you will have to look elsewhere for your pocket-book."

The man went off, muttering that he had no doubt it was his; but he saw clearly that he had failed. However, he was not yet at the end of his resources. At the corner of Broadway and Fulton Streets he was greeted by another young man of similar appearance.

"Well, Jack, what luck?"

"I came away as poor as I went."

"Then you couldn't hit the description?"

"No, he was too many for me."

"Anyway, you found out something. Give me a few hints, and I'll try my luck."

" He asked me if the pocket-book was brown, and I said yes. That's wrong. You'd better say it's black, or some other color."

" All right. I'll remember. What else did he ask you?"

" Where I lost it."

" What did you say?"

" In Nassau or Fulton Street, I couldn't say which."

" Was that wrong?"

" I don't know, he didn't say."

" What next?"

" He asked how much money there was. I said from fifty to seventy-five dollars, though I afterwards said there might be over eighty."

" That's too wide a margin. I think I'll say a hundred and fifty, more or less."

" That might do."

" As soon as I've smoked out my cigar, I'll go up."

" Good luck to you, Bob. Mind we are to divide, if you get it."

" You shall have a third."

" No, half."

" I'll see about it ; but I haven't got it yet."

In a few moments the superintendent received a second applicant.

" Good-morning, sir," said the individual named " Bob." " You've found a pocket-book, I think."

" Yes."

" I'm glad of it. I lost mine yesterday, with a pretty stiffish sum of money in it. I suppose one of your newsboys picked it up."

" Did you lose it in this street?"

" Yes, I expect so. I was coming from the Fulton Ferry in a great hurry, and there was a big hole in my pocket, that I didn't know of. I had just got the money for a horse that I sold to a man over there."

" Will you describe the pocket-book? What color was it?"

" Black, that is to say, not perhaps exactly black, but it might be called black," said Bob, getting over this question as well as he could.

" Very well. Now for the amount of money in the pocket-book."

" A hundred and fifty dollars, more or less," said Bob, boldly.

"In three bills of fifty dollars each?" asked the superintendent.

"Yes, precisely," said Bob, eagerly. "That was what was paid for the horse I sold."

"Then I regret to say that the pocket-book in my possession cannot be yours. When I find one answer ing your description as to color and contents, I will hold it at your disposal."

"Sold!" muttered Bob to himself, as he slunk downstairs without another word.

He rejoined his confederate, who was waiting for him at the corner, and informed him in expressive language that it was "no go."

"P'r'aps, if we'd consulted a medium, we might have found out all about the color and amount," sug gested Jack.

"Don't you believe it," said Bob. "If the mediums could tell that, they'd be after it themselves. Where's your 'Herald'? We may get or better at some other place."

They found an advertisement of a diamond ring found, and started in pursuit of the finder. As Jack said, "We might get it, you know; and if we don't, there's no harm done."

Mr. O'Connor had various other applications for the pocket-book, of which we will only describe one.

A woman dressed in black presented herself about noon.

"Is this the superintendent?" she asked.

"Yes, ma'am."

"I came to see you about that pocket-book you advertise. I am a widow with six children, and I have hard work to get along. Yesterday I sent out my oldest boy to pay the rent; but he is a careless boy, and I suppose he got to playing in the street, and it fell out of his pocket. It was a great loss to me, and a widow's blessings shall rest upon you, sir, if you restore it. My boy's name is Henry, and I can bring you the best recommendations that I am a respectable woman, and my word can be relied upon."

This speech was delivered with such volubility, and with such a steady flow of words, that the superintendent had no opportunity of interrupting her.

"May I ask your name, madam?" he said **at** length.

"My name is Manson, sir, Mrs. Manson. **My** husband was an honest man, — he was a blacksmith, — but he was tock down sudden with a fever about three years ago, that carried him off, and left me to get along as well as I could with my family of children. I ought to be back now ; so if you'll give it to me, **you** you can take what you like for the advertising, **and** to pay you for your trouble."

"You are a little too fast, Mrs. Manson. **How** am I to know that the pocket-book is yours?"

"I'll bring my son Henry to prove that he lost **the** pocket-book when he was going to pay the rent."

"That will not be necessary. All you will **have** to do will be to describe the pocket-book and its contents, and, if your description is correct, I **will** take it for granted that it belongs to you, and give **i** to you at once."

"Describe it, sir?"

"Yes, what was the color?"

"I can't justly say, sir, for it was Henry's **pocket**

9

book," said Mrs. Manson, hesitating; "but I think it was black."

"And how much money was there in it?"

"Thirty dollars," said the widow, with a little hesitation.

"Then the pocket-book isn't yours.   Good morning, madam."

"It's hard upon a poor widow to lose her money, sir, and then have the finder refuse to give it up," whined Mrs. Manson.

"It would be, no doubt; but it would be equally hard for the real owner of the money for me to give it to the wrong person."

"But I think the pocket-book is mine."

"You are mistaken, madam."

Mrs. Manson, who, by the way, was not a widow, and didn't have six children as represented, went away crestfallen.

A week passed, and the money still remained in the hands of Mr. O'Connor.   Numerous applicants had been drawn by the advertisment, one or two of whom had met with genuine losses, but the greater part were adventurers who trusted to lucky guessing to get hold of money that did not belong to them. The advertisements of money lost were also carefully examined daily; but there was none that answered to the sum found by the newsboy.

"I am beginning to think," said Mr. O'Connor, after a week had passed, "that you won't find an owner for this money, Rufus. What do you intend to do with it?"

"I'll put it in some bank, sir," said the newsboy, promptly. "I don't need to use it at present, but I may some time. It'll be something for me to fall back upon, if I get sick."

"I am glad you do not mean to live upon it. I was afraid it might encourage you to idleness."

"No, sir, it won't do that," said Rough and Ready, promptly. "I'm not such a fool as that. I've got a little sister to take care of, and I've thought sometimes, 'What if I should get sick?' but with this money, I shan't feel afraid. I think it'll make me work harder. I should like to add something to it if I could."

"That is the right way to talk, Rufus," said the superintendent, approvingly. "I think you are a good boy, and I shall be glad to help you with advice, or in any other way, whenever you need it. I wish you could get an education; it would help you along in life hereafter."

"I am studying every evening, sir," said the newsboy. "Miss Manning, a friend of mine, that my sister boards with, is helping me. I hope to be something higher than a newsboy some time."

The superintendent warmly applauded his determination, and a week later gave the pocket-book up to Rough and Ready, feeling that every reasonable effort to find an owner had been tried.

CHAPTER XII.

A VISIT TO GREENWOOD CEMETERY.

ONE day Rough and Ready came to see his sister, and displayed a bank-book on one of the city savings-banks, containing an entry of three hundred dollars to his credit.

"What do you think of that, Rosie?" he said. "Don't you think I am rich?"

"I don't see anything but a little book," said Rose, who knew nothing of the way in which savings-banks were conducted. "There isn't any money in it," she continued, turning over the leaves with the expectation of finding some bills folded between them.

"You don't understand it, Rose. That little book is worth three hundred dollars."

"Three hundred dollars! Why, I wouldn't give five cents for it."

The newsboy laughed. "It shows that I have

three hundred dollars in the bank, which they will pay me whenever I want it."

"That is nice," said Rose. "I am so glad you are rich, Rufie."

"Then you have heard nothing of the owner of the money, Rufus?" said Miss Manning.

"No, I have heard nothing. Mr. O'Connor says I shall be right in keeping the money now, as I have tried to find the owner, and cannot."

"What do you propose to do with it?"

"I shall keep it in the bank at present, until I need it. But there is one thing I would like to do, Miss Manning."

"What is that?"

"I would like to make you a present, — a dress, or shawl, or whatever you need most."

"Thank you, Rufus; you are very kind," said the seamstress; "but I would prefer that you would leave the money untouched. Since I made the arrangement with you about Rose, I am doing much better than I did before, and I feel much better, because I have more sustaining food. I feel now as if I could afford to take a little time to sew for myself. I bought a dress-pattern yesterday, and I shall make it up next week."

" But I should like very much to make you a present, Miss Manning."

" So you shall, Rufus, whenever you have a thousand dollars laid aside. At present I do not need anything, and I would rather you would keep your money."

To this resolution Miss Manning adhered, in spite of the newsboy's urgent persuasion. She knew very well that three hundred dollars, though it seemed a large sum to him, would rapidly melt away if it was once broken in upon, and she wished it to be kept as a " nest-egg," and an encouragement for future accumulations.

" At any rate," said Rufus, " I want to celebrate my good luck, and I want you to help me do it. Let us go to-morrow afternoon to Greenwood Cemetery. I think Rose will like it, and as it is a beautiful place it will be pleasant for us all."

" Very well," said the seamstress, " I will agree to that, if you will wait till I have finished my dress,

I think I can have it done, so that we can go on Wednesday afternoon. Will that do?"

"Yes, that will suit me very well. I hope it will be a pleasant day."

"If it is not, we can defer it to the next day."

It will need to be explained that Rufus had already five dollars in the bank previous to his coming into possession of the contents of the pocket-book. That had originally contained three hundred dollars, but five dollars had been taken out to defray the expenses of advertising in the "Herald."

When Rose was informed of the contemplated excursion, she was filled with delight. The poor child had had very little pleasure or variety, and the excursion, brief as it was, she anticipated with eager enjoyment.

The day opened auspiciously. The early morning hours the newsboy devoted to his business, being unwilling to lose a day's earnings. At eleven o'clock he came to Miss Manning's lodgings. "Well, I am through with my day's work," he said. "How much do you think I have earned?"

"Seventy-five cents?" said the seamstress, inquiringly.

" A dollar and twenty cents," he said.

" You have been very smart. What a number of papers you must have sold ! "

" I didn't make it all that way. There were two boys who were hard up, and hadn't any blacking-brushes ; so I bought them some, and they are to pay me ten cents a day, each of them, for a month, then I shall let them keep the brushes."

" Do the boys often make such arrangements?"

" No, they generally go *whacks.* The boy who borrows agrees to pay half his earnings to the boy that sets him up in business."

" That is rather a hard bargain."

" Yes, I didn't want to charge so much. So I only charged ten cents a day."

" That will pay you a good profit ; but how do you know but the boys will keep the brushes, and won't pay you anything?"

" Oh, they won't do that. They'll keep their promises, or nobody would help 'em next time they get hard up."

Miss Manning had prepared an early dinner, to which they all sat down. This was soon despatched, and they set out together for the South Ferry, from which cars ran to the cemetery.

They reached the ferry about noon, and at once crossed over. Rose enjoyed the ride upon the boat, for, though New York is surrounded by ferries, she had hardly ever ridden on a ferry-boat.

" I wish we didn't get out so quick," she said.

" Do you like being on the water, Rosie?"

" Ever so much," replied the little girl.

" Then we will take a longer excursion some day soon. We can go to Staten Island. That will be six miles each way."

" That will be nice. I hope we can go soon."

They soon reached the Brooklyn side, and disembarked with the throng of fellow-passengers. A car was waiting the boat's arrival, on which they saw " GREENWOOD " printed.

" Jump on board quick," said Rough and Ready, " or you won't get seats."

Miss Manning barely got a seat. She took Rose in her lap, and the newsboy stood out on the platform with the conductor. The ride was a pleasant one to all three, but no incidents happened worth noting.

When Rufus settled the fare, the conductor said jo-
cosely, " Your wife and child, I suppose?"

" No," said the newsboy, "all my children are
grown up and out of the way. They don't give me
any trouble."

" That's where you're lucky," said the conductor.
" It's more than I can say."

" Have you a family? "

" Yes, I have a wife and four children, and precious hard work I find it to support them on my
small wages. But it's no use asking any more."

" That's my sister, the little girl I mean," said
Rufus. " The other is a friend who looks after her.
I have to support her; but that's only one, while you
have five."

" She looks like a nice little girl. She is about
the size of my oldest girl."

" She's a dear little sister," said the newsboy,
warmly. " I should feel very lonely without her."

He little thought as he spoke that the loneliness to
which he referred was speedily to come upon him.
But we will not anticipate.

They got out at the entrance of the cemetery, and

entered the grounds. Greenwood Cemetery, of which all my readers have probably heard, is very extensive, the grounds comprising over three hundred acres. It is situated about two and a half miles from the South Ferry, on what is now known as Gowanus Heights. Its elevated position enables it to command charming views of the bay and harbor of New York; with its islands and forts, the twin cities of New York and Brooklyn, the New Jersey shore, the long lines of city wharves, with their forests of masts, and an extensive view of the ocean. The numerous and beautiful trees crowning the elevations, the costly monuments, the winding paths, so intersecting each other as almost to make a labyrinth, render this a charming spot, and death assumes a less repulsive aspect amid such surroundings.

"How beautiful it is!" said Miss Manning, gazing about her thoughtfully. "I have never been here before."

"I never came but once," said the newsboy, "and that was a good while ago."

Little Rose was charmed, and darted first into one path, then into another, and was about to pluck some flowers, until she was told that this was against the regulations.

" What a lot of dead people live here ! " she said, as from a little height they saw white stones and monuments rising on every side.

" She has used the right word, after all, Rufus," said Miss Manning ; " for death is only the introduction to another life. I sometimes think that those whose bodies lie here are not wholly insensible to the beauty by which they are surrounded."

" I don't know," said the newsboy, " I never thought much about it till mother died. I wish she had been buried here. I think it would be a comfort to me. Poor mother ! she had a hard life ; " and he sighed. " I want Rose to have a happier one."

" Let us hope she will. Have you heard anything of Mr. Martin lately ? "

She carefully avoided using the word " stepfather " for she had observed that even this recognition of relationship was distasteful to the boy, who had imbibed a bitter prejudice against the man who had wrecked his mother's happiness, and undoubtedly abridged her life by several years.

"No, I have not seen him since the day after I took Rose away from Leonard Street. I think he cannot be in the city, or he would have come round to where I was selling papers. I expected he would be round before to ask me for some money."

"What do you think has become of him?"

"Maybe he has gone back into the country. I hope he has, for I should feel safer about Rose."

Here the conversation closed for the time. They rambled on without any particular aim, wherever fancy dictated. They came upon most of the notable monuments, including that of the sea-captain, and that of Miss Canda, the young heiress, who, dying by a violent accident, with no one to inherit her wealth, it was decided that it should all be expended upon a costly monument, which has ever since been one of the chief ornaments of the cemetery.

At length they began to think of returning, but had some difficulty at first in finding their way to the gate, so perplexing is the maze of paths.

"I don't know but we shall have to stay here all night," said Rufus. "How should you like that, Rose?"

"I wouldn't care," said the little girl. "I think the grass would make a nice soft bed."

But to this necessity they were not reduced, as after a while they emerged into a broad path that led down to the gateway. They passed through it, and got on board a horse-car.

"I think we will go to Fulton Ferry this time," said Rough and Ready. "It will give us a little change."

He did not realize to what misfortune this choice of his would lead, or he would not have made it; but we cannot foresee what our most trifling decisions may lead to. In due time they got on board the Fulton ferry-boat, and went into the ladies' cabin. They didn't see a man who followed their motions with an eager gaze, mingled with malice. It was James Martin, who saw Rose now for the first time since she was taken from Leonard Street by her brother.

"This is lucky!" he muttered to himself. "I will find out where she lives, and then it will be a pretty tight cage, or I shall be able to secure the bird."

But there was danger that, if he followed in person, the newsboy might look back, and, perceiving his

design, foil it by going in the wrong direction. **He**
quickly decided what to do.   There was a half-grown
boy near by whom he knew slightly.

" Here, boy," said he, " do you want to earn half **a**
dollar?"

" Yes," said the boy.

" Then you must follow some people whom **I** will
point out to you, and find out where they live.   **Don't**
let them see that they are followed."

" All right, sir."

When Rough and Ready got out of the boat with
his two companions, they were followed at a little distance by this boy; but of this they were quite unaware.

CHAPTER XIII.

ROSE AND HER ENEMY.

JAMES MARTIN waited at the Fulton Ferry for the return of his emissary. But he had to wait a long time, as the lodgings occupied by Miss Manning and little Rose were rather more than a mile distant, and their progress was somewhat delayed by their stopping to listen to a little Italian boy and his sister, who were singing near the head of Fulton Street. Then there was a difficulty in crossing Broadway, on account of the stream of vehicles. Owing to these causes, it was an hour and a quarter before the messenger returned. James Martin had about made up his mind that the boy had given up the quest, and was starting away in vexation and disappointment, just as he appeared in sight.

"Well, you've been gone long enough," he said, roughly. "Why didn't you stay all night?"

"I came as quick as I could. It's a long ways,"

10

said the boy. "Then they stopped two or three times."

"Did you find out where they lived?" asked Martin, eagerly.

'Yes, I followed 'em clear to the door."

" Where is it?"

" Where's the half dollar you promised me?" said the boy, with commendable caution.

"I'll give it to you when you've told me where it is."

" I want it first."

" Do you think I won't give it to you?" demanded Martin, angrily.

" Maybe you will, and maybe you won't. I never saw you before."

" I'll give you the money as soon as you tell me."

"It's No. 125 Centre Street."

"All right, my lad, I'll pay you when I get ready as long as you've made such a fuss about it."

" Well," said the boy, coolly, " I guess you won't make any more out of it than I do."

" Why not?" asked Martin suspiciously.

" Because I've told you the wrong street and number."

" Is that so? "

" If you don't believe it, go to 125 Centre Street,
and see if you can find them."

" You're a young rascal," said Martin, angry at
being foiled.

" Maybe I am ; but I don't mean to be cheated by
you or any other man.'"

" I've a good mind to give you a thrashing."

" You'd better if you want to sleep in the station-
house to-night," returned the boy, not in the least
alarmed.

" So you were going to tell me the wrong place,
and take my money, were you? "

" No ; if you'd given me the money, I'd have told
you right afterwards."

" Well, here's your money," said Martin, taking
out fifty cents.

" I want seventy-five cents now."

" What for? "

" Because you tried to cheat me."

" Then I won't give you anything."

"All right. Then you must find out for yourself where they live."

"Come, boy, don't be foolish. Here's your fifty cents."

"Keep it yourself till there's twenty-five more."

Further effort proving unavailing, James Martin recalled the boy, who had already started to go, and very unwillingly complied with his demand.

"Well," said the boy, depositing the money carefully in his pocket, "now I'll tell you. It's No. — Franklin Street, near the North River."

"Are you telling me the truth?" asked Martin, suspiciously, for he would never have thought of this quarter.

"Yes, it's the truth. If you don't believe it, you can go and see for yourself."

"Franklin Street!" repeated Martin to himself. "Perhaps it's true. The boy's a deep one. He thought I wouldn't find him out there. Perhaps he'll find himself mistaken. I'd like to see him when he finds the girl gone."

James Martin, not relying wholly on the boy's information, determined to go round and find the place indicated, and see if he couldn't ascertain definitely whether it was correct. If so, he would lay his plans accordingly.

Following up this determination, twenty minutes later found him standing in front of the house. But he could not, without inquiring, obtain the desired information, and this he hardly liked to do, lest it should be reported to Rough and Ready, and so put him on his guard.

He stood undecided what to do ; but chance favored him. While he was considering, he saw the newsboy himself come up the street and enter the house, with a loaf of bread under his arm. He was just returning from a bakery near by, and the bread was to form a part of the supper to which all three brought excellent appetites.

James Martin crouched back in a door-way, in order to escape observation, at the same time pulling his hat over his eyes. The precaution, however, proved unnecessary, for the newsboy never looked across the street, and was far enough from suspecting the danger that menaced the little household. He was thinking rather of the nice supper, — a little better

10

than usual, — which was being prepared in honor of the holiday, and thinking how much more pleasantly they were situated than in the room at Leonard Street, on the other side of the city.

"It's all right!" muttered Martin to himself with satisfaction. "The boy told me the truth, and I don't mind the seventy-five cents, as long as I've found out where they live. They'll find I aint so easily fooled as I might be. A day or two'll tell the story."

He had learned all he wished to know, and walked back to Broadway, where it is unnecessary to follow him.

The next day Rose and Miss Manning were sitting together in the neat little room to which both had become attached. Miss Manning was sewing as usual. Rose was sitting on a stool at her feet, with her eyes fixed on a small reading-book.

"I think I know my lesson, Miss Manning," she said at last, raising her eyes.

"Very well, Rose, I am ready to hear you."

The seamstress laid down her work, and Rose,

standing by her side, read the lesson to her without a mistake.

"Didn't I say it well, Miss Manning?" she asked, proudly.

"Yes, Rose, you are doing famously; I am quite proud of my pupil."

"I shall soon get through my book. Then Rufie will have to buy me another."

"I have no doubt he will be very glad to do so, Rose. He is very anxious that you should get along fast."

"Isn't he a good boy, Miss Manning?"

"Yes, he is a very kind, considerate brother."

"I like it so much better than when I lived with — Mr. Martin. Do you think I shall ever see him again, Miss Manning?"

"I cannot tell, Rose. I hope not; for I do not think you would be happy with him."

"He used to drink rum, and it made him so cross I used to be afraid of him."

"Rum ruins a great many people, Rose."

"I don't see how anybody can like it," said the little girl. "Once fath — I mean Mr. Martin,

brought some home in a bottle, and when he **was**
out, I thought I would just taste a little — ”

“ O Rose ! ”

“ Only a very little, a tiny spoonful, to see **how it**
tasted. But it was so strong, and tasted so bad, **I**
could not swallow it. I don’t see how anybody **can**
like it.”

“ Yes, Rose, it does seem strange. But I am
going to ask you to go on a little errand for me.”

“ I should like to go,” said the little girl, jumping
up. “ What is it, Miss Manning ? ”

“ I need a spool of cotton. You know the little
store round the corner.”

“ Lindsay’s ? ”

“ Yes. I should like to have you go there and buy
me another spool, the same number as this. I will
give you the spool, so that you can show it to the
man behind the counter.”

“ Yes, Miss Manning.”

“ Here are ten cents. You can bring me back **the**
change. . If you want to, you can stop at the candy-
shop, and buy a stick of candy out of what is
left.”

"Oh, thank you, Miss Manning. Shan't I buy you a stick too?"

"No, Rose, I have got over my love for candy."

"Didn't you use to like it when you were a little girl?"

"Yes, Rose; but now make haste, for I have only a needleful of cotton left, and I want to finish this work to-night, if I can."

Rose put on her bonnet, and went downstairs, proud of the commission with which she was intrusted. She was actually going shopping, just as grown women do, and this gave her a feeling of dignity which made her carry her little form with unusual erectness. She little suspected that the danger which her brother and herself most dreaded lay in wait for her in the street beneath; that she was about to be torn from the pleasant home which she had begun to enjoy so much. Nor did Miss Manning suspect to what peril she was exposing her young charge, and what grief she was unconsciously laying up for Rufus and herself.

James Martin was lurking near the house, and had been lounging about there for three or four hours

He had notified his employer in the morning that he had business in New York, and should be unable to work that day. He had also given notice to his landlady that he expected to bring his daughter home that night, and he wanted her to prepare accommodations for her.

With the design of procuring her he had come over and repaired to Franklin Street; but Rose and Miss Manning seldom stirred out in the morning, and he had watched and waited in vain until now. He had made several visits to a neighboring groggery and indulged in potations which helped to while away the time, but he was getting very impatient, when, to his great joy, he saw Rose come out upon the sidewalk, *and alone,* which was better still. He had made up his mind to claim her, even if she were accompanied by Miss Manning; but this might excite a disturbance, and he knew there would be danger of interference from the police, which he did not court. So he considered it a remarkable stroke of good luck when he saw Rose coming out alone.

"There she is," he said to himself. "I'll soon nab her. But I wonder where she is going."

He might have seized her at once, but he thought it best not to do so. Very likely there might be somebody who might witness the seizure, who would know that she was living with Miss Manning, and might be inclined to interfere. He thought it would be better to follow her a little distance, and effect the capture in another locality.

Rose pursued her way, unconscious of the danger that menaced her. She entered the store, made her purchase, and it wasn't till she had gone a little away from the store that she felt a heavy hand upon her shoulder, and, looking round, to her indescribable dismay and terror, recognized her stepfather.

CHAPTER XIV.

ROSE KIDNAPPED.

"So I've found you at last," said James Martin, looking grimly at Rose, bending over so that the fumes of his breath, tainted with liquor, seemed to scorch her innocent cheek.

"Let me go," said Rose, terrified and ready to cry.

"Let you go!" repeated Martin, with a sneer. "Is that all the welcome you've got for me, after I've taken the pains to come clear over from Brooklyn to find you? No, I can't let you go; I'm your father, and you must go with me."

"I can't, indeed I can't," said Rose, in distress "I want to stay with Rufie and Miss Manning."

"I can't allow it. I'm your father, and I'm responsible for you. Your brother aint fit to have charge of you. Come along."

He seized her by the shoulder, and began to push her along.

"I don't want to go," said Rose, crying. "I don't want to leave Rufie."

"I don't care what you want," said Martin, roughly. "You've got to come with me, anyhow. As for your brother, I don't want him. He'd be trying to kidnap you again. I might have put him in prison for it; but I'll let him go this time, if you don't make any fuss."

"What is the matter?" asked a policeman, who came up as Rose was struggling weakly in the grasp of her stepfather. "What are you pulling along the little girl for?"

"Because she won't come without," said Martin. "She ran away from home with her brother a few weeks ago, and I've just found her."

"Is she your child?"

"Yes."

"Is that true?" asked the policeman, not particularly prepossessed in Martin's favor by his personal appearance, his face being unusually inflamed by his

morning potations. His question was of course
directed to Rose.

" No, I aint his child now," said Rose. " Rufie has
the care of me."

" And who is Rufie?"

" He is my brother."

" He's a young rascal," said Martin, " up to all
sorts of mischief. He'll lie and steal, and anything
else that's bad. He aint fit to have charge of
Rose."

" It isn't true," said the little girl, indignantly
" He doesn't lie nor steal. He's the best boy that
ever lived."

" I haven't anything to do with that," said the
policeman. " The question is, is this your father?"

" He was mother's husband," said Rose, reluctantly.

" Then he is your stepfather."

" Don't let him take me away," said Rose, im-
ploringly.

" If he's your stepfather, I can't stop him. But,
hark you, my man, I advise you to be kind to the
little girl. If you are not, I hope she'll run away

from you. You look as if you'd been drinking pretty hard this morning."

" It's the trouble I've had about her that made me drink," said Martin, apologetically. " I was afraid she wasn't taken good care of. Come along now, Rose. He says you must go."

"Let me go and speak to Miss Manning first," entreated Rose. " I've got a spool of cotton I've just bought for her."

" I'm not such a fool as that," said Martin. " I've looked for you long enough, and now I've got you I mean to hold on to you."

" But Miss Manning won't know where I am," pleaded Rose.

" It's none of her business where you **are**. **She** aint no relation of yours."

" But she's been very kind to me."

" She was kind enough to keep you away from me, she hasn't anything to do with you, and I don't mean she shall ever see you again."

Poor Rose ! the thought that she was to be forever separated from her kind friend, Miss Manning, smote

her with a sharp sorrow, and she began to cry bitterly.

"Stop your whimpering," said Martin, roughly,
" or I'll give you something to cry about."

But, even with this threat hanging over her, Rose
could not check the flow of her tears. Those persons
whom they met looked with sympathy at the pretty
little girl, who was roughly pulled along by the red-
faced, rough-looking man ; and more than one would
have been glad to interfere if he had felt authorized
to do so.

James Martin did not relish the public attention
drawn to them by Rose's tears, for he knew instinc-
tively that the sympathy would be with her, and not
with himself. As soon as possible he got the child
on board a horse-car bound for the South Ferry.
This was something of an improvement, for he was
no longer obliged to drag her along. But even in the
cars her tears continued to flow.

"What's the matter with your little girl?" asked
a kind, motherly-looking woman, who had a daughter
at home about Rose's age, and whose sympathies

were therefore more readily excited by the appearance of distress in the child's face.

" She's been behaving badly, ma'am," said Martin.

" She doesn't look like a bad child," said the good woman, kindly.

" You can't tell by her looks," said Martin. " Maybe you'd think, to look at her, that she was one of the best children out ; but she's very troublesome."

" I'm sorry to hear that. You should try to be good, my dear," said the woman, gently.

Rose didn't reply, but continued to shed tears.

" She's got a brother that's a regular bad one," continued Mr. Martin. " He's a little scamp, if there ever was one. Would you believe it, ma'am, he induced his sister to run away from home some weeks ago, and ever since I've been hunting all around to find her?"

" Is it possible?" exclaimed the other, interested " Where did you find her, if I may be allowed to ask?"

" In a low place, in the western part of the city," said Mr. Martin. " It wasn't a fit place for a child like her. Her brother carried her away from a good home, just out of spite, because he got angry with me."

" It must have made you feel very anxious."

" Yes, " said Mr. Martin, pathetically. " It worried me so I couldn't sleep nights. I've been hunting night and day for her ever since, but it's only to-day that I got track of her. She's crying now because she didn't want to leave the woman her brother placed her with."

" I'm sorry to hear it. My dear, you will be better off at home than among strangers. Don't you think you will? "

" No, I shan't," said Rose. " Miss Manning was a good woman, and was very kind to me."

" She isn't old enough to judge," said Martin, shrugging his shoulders.

" No, of course not. Where do you live? "

" In Brooklyn."

" Well, good-by ; I get out here."

" Good-by, ma'am. I hope you won't have so much trouble with your children as I have."

" I am sure your little girl will be better when she gets home."

' I hope so, ma'am."

Rose did not speak. She was too much distressed, and, child as she was, she had an instinctive feeling that her stepfather was false and hypocritical, and she did not feel spirit enough to contradict his assertions about herself and Rufus.

At length they reached the ferry, and embarked on the ferry-boat.

Rose no longer tried to get away. In the first place, she was now so far away from home that she would not have known her way back. Besides, she saw that Mr. Martin was determined to carry her with him, and that resistance would be quite useless, so in silent misery she submitted herself to what it seemed impossible to escape.

They got into the cars on the other side, and the trip passed without incident.

"We get out here," said Mr. Martin, when they had been riding about half an hour.

Rose meekly obeyed his summons, and followed him out of the car.

"Now, young lady," said Mr. Martin, sternly, "I

am going to give you a piece of advice.   Are **you** listening?"

" Yes," said Rose, dispiritedly.

" Then you had better give up snivelling at once It aint going to do you any good.   Maybe, if you behave well, I'll let your brother see you after a while, but if you kick up a fuss you'll never see him again in the world.   Do you understand?"

" Yes."

" I hope you do.   Anyway, you'd better.   I live over here now.   I've took board for you and myself in the house of a woman that's got a girl about as big as you.   If you aint foolish you'll have a good time playing with her."

" I want to see Rufie," moaned Rose.

" Well, you can't, and the sooner you make up your mind to that the better.   Here we are."

He opened the front door of the shabby boarding house, and said to the servant whom he met in the entry, " Where's Mrs. Waters?"

" I'll call her directly, if you'd like to see her "

" Yes, I want to see her."

Mrs. Waters shortly appeared, her face red with heat, from the kitchen.

" I've brought my little girl along, as I told you," said Martin.

" So this is your little girl, is it? She's a nice child," said Mrs. Waters, rather surprised to find that a man of Mr. Martin's unpromising exterior had so attractive a child.

" No, she isn't," said Martin, shaking his head. " She's very badly behaved. I've let her stay in New York with some relations, and she didn't want to come back and see father. She's been making a great fuss about it."

" She'll feel better to-morrow," said **Mrs. Waters.** " How old is she?"

" Seven years old."

" Just the age of my Fanny."

" You said you could let her occupy the same bed with your little girl."

" Yes, they can sleep together. Fanny will like to have a girl of her own age to play with. Wait a minute, — I'll call her."

Fanny Waters was a short, dumpy little girl, of

extreme plainness. Rose looked at her, but didn't appear to feel much attracted.

"You can go out into the back yard together and play," said Mrs. Waters; "only mind and don't get into any mischief."

"Wait a minute," said Mr. Martin, calling Rose aside, "I want to speak to her a minute. If," he continued, addressing the child, "you try to run away, I'll go over to New York, and shoot your brother through the head with a pistol. So mind what you're about."

Rose listened in silent terror, for she thought her stepfather might really do as he threatened, and it had a greater effect upon her than if he had threatened harm to herself.

James Martin witnessed with satisfaction the effect produced in the pale, scared face of the child, and he said to himself, "I don't think she'll run away in a hurry."

CHAPTER XV.

INTRODUCES A DISTINGUISHED PERSONAGE.

"'Times,' 'Herald,' 'Tribune,' 'World'!" cried Rough and Ready, from his old place in front of the "Times" building. "All the news that's going, for only four cents! That's cheap enough, isn't it? Have a paper, sir?"

"I don't know. Is there any particular news this morning?" asked the individual addressed.

"Yes, sir, lots of it. You will find ten cents' worth in every one of the papers, which will give you a clear profit of six cents on your investment. Which will you have?"

"Let me look at a paper a minute, and I'll see."

"I don't do business that way," said the newsboy; "not since one morning when I let an old gentleman look at a paper just for a minute. He read it for half an hour, and then returned it, sayin' there wasn't much in it, and he guessed he wouldn't buy."

" Well, here's your money. Give me the ' Times,' "
said the other.

" Here you are ! " said the newsboy, pocketing the
money, and placing a " Times " in the hand of the
purchaser.

" Give me the ' Herald,' " said another.

Unfolding the paper, he glanced his eye over it,
and said, in evident disappointment, " I heard there
was a railroad accident somewhere, with about fifty
persons killed and wounded ; but I don't see it anywhere."

" I'm sorry you're disappointed," said the newsboy. " It's soothin' to the feelings to read about a
smash-up, with lots of persons killed and wounded.
Just come along to-morrow mornin', and I guess
you'll find what you want."

" What makes you think so ? " asked the customer,
suspiciously.

" If you won't mention it," said Rough and Ready,
lowering his voice, " I don't mind telling you that
the ' Herald ' has sent up a reporter to put a big rock
on the Erie Road, and throw off the afternoon train
As he will be on the spot, he can give a full report.

exclusive for the 'Herald'! Then again, the 'Times' and 'Tribune' are arrangin' to get up some 'horrid murders.' Maybe they'll have 'em in to-morrow's paper. You'd better come round, and buy 'em all. I'll make a discount to a wholesale customer."

"It's my belief that you're a humbug," said the disappointed customer.

"Thank you, sir," said Rough and Ready; "I've been takin' lessons of Barnum, only I haven't made so much money yet."

The next customer asked for the "Tribune."

"Here it is, sir."

"Did you ever see Mr. Greeley?" he inqured. "I live in the country, and I have often thought I should like to see so intrepid a champion of the people's rights."

"There he is now," said the newsboy, pointing to a somewhat portly man, who had just got out of a horse-car.

"You don't say so!" ejaculated the country reader of the "Tribune." "I should like to go and shake hands with him, but he might take it as too great a liberty. I didn't know he was so stout."

"Go ahead!" said the newsboy. "He won'; mind. He's used to it."

"I think I will. I should like to tell the folks a home that I had shaken hands with Horace Greeley.'

Now it happened that the personage who had been pointed out as Horace Greeley was really no other than Mr. Barnum himself, the illustrious showman. The newsboy was well aware of this, and was led to make the statement by his desire to see a little fun. I shall not attempt to justify him in this deception; but I have undertaken to set Rough and Ready before the reader as he was, not as he ought to be, and, though a good boy in the main, he was not without faults.

Mr. Greeley's admirer walked up to Mr. Barnum, and grasped his hand cordially.

"Sir," he said, "I hope you will excuse the liberty I am taking, but I couldn't help addressing you."

"I am glad to meet you, sir," said Mr. Barnum, courteously. "Perhaps I have met you before, but I meet so many people that I cannot always remember faces."

"No, sir, we have never met before, but your fame has reached our village; indeed, I may say, it has spread all over the country, and when I was told who you were I could not help coming up and telling you how much we all sympathize with you in your philanthropic efforts."

Mr. Barnum looked somewhat perplexed. He was not altogether certain whether his temperance lectures were referred to, or his career as manager of the Museum. He answered therefore rather vaguely, "I try to do something to make the world happier. I am very glad my efforts are appreciated."

"Yes, sir, you may be certain they are appreciated throughout the length and breadth of the land," said the other, fervently.

"You are very kind," said Barnum; "but I am afraid you will not get all to agree with you. There are some who do not view me so favorably."

"Of course. Such is always the fate of the philanthropist. There are some, no doubt, who decry you, but their calumnies are unavailable. 'Truth crushed to earth will rise again.' I need not continue the quotation."

" You are certainly very complimentary, Mr. ——; perhaps you will oblige me with your name."

" Nathan Bedloe. I keep a seminary in the country. I have read the ' Tribune ' for years, Mr. Greeley, and have found in your luminous editorials the most satisfactory exposition of the principles which I profess."

Mr. Barnum's eyes distended with astonishment as he caught the name Greeley, and his facial muscles twitched a little.

" How did you know me? " he asked.

" That newsboy pointed you out to me," said the other, indicating Rough and Ready, who was watch-ing with interest the conversation between the two.

" Yes, the newsboys know me," said Barnum. " So you like the ' Tribune'? "

" Yes, sir, it is an admirable paper. I would as soon do without my dinner as without it."

" I am very glad you like it," said Barnum ; " but I fear my own contributions to it (referring to the advertisement of the Museum) are not worthy of such kind compliments. I must bid you good-morning, at present, as my engagements are numerous."

" I can easily believe it, Mr. Greeley. Good-by, sir. Thank you for your kind reception of an humble stranger."

There was another shaking of hands, and Mr. Bedloe departed under the firm conviction that he had .seen and talked with Horace Greeley.

Three minutes later, Rough and Ready felt a hand upon his shoulder. Lifting up his eyes, he recognized Mr. Barnum.

" Do you know me ? " asked the latter.

" Yes, sir, you are Mr. Barnum."

" Were you the boy who pointed me out as Horace Greeley ? "

" Yes, sir," said Rufus, laughing ; " but I didn't think the man would believe it."

" He thinks so still," said Barnum. " I don't think there's much personal resemblance between me and the editor of the ' Tribune,' " he continued, meditatively.

" No, sir, not much."

" Don't do it again, my lad. It's wrong to humbug people, you know. By the way, do you ever come to the Museum?"

"Yes, sir."

"Well, your joke is worth something. Here is a season ticket for three months."

He handed the newsboy, as he spoke, a slip of paper on which was written: —

"Admit the bearer to any performance in the Museum during the next three months.   P. T. BARNUM."

"I got off better than I expected," thought Rough and Ready. "I didn't know but both of 'em would get mad, and be down upon me. I wish he'd given me a ticket for three, and I'd have taken Miss Manning and Rose along with me."

As he thought of Rose, it was with a feeling of satisfaction that she was so well provided for. He had the utmost confidence in Miss Manning, and he saw that a mutual affection had sprung up between her and his little sister.

"It'll be jolly when Rose grows up, and can keep house for me," he said to himself. "I hope I'll be in some good business then. Selling papers will do very well now, but I want to do something else after a while. I wonder whether that three hundred dollars I've got in the bank wouldn't set me up in some kind of business."

While these thoughts were passing through his mind, he still kept crying his papers, and presently he had sold the last one. It was still comparatively early, and he thought he would look about a little to see if there was no chance of earning a little extra money by running on an errand.

After a while he was commissioned to carry a message to Twenty-Second Street, for which he was to receive twenty-five cents, and his car fares.

" I'll walk back," he thought, " and in that way I'll save six cents out of the fares."

The walk being a long one, he was absent a considerable time, especially as he stopped for a while at an auction on Broadway. At last he reached his old stand, and was thinking of buying some evening papers, when he heard his name called in a tone of anxiety.

Turning suddenly, he recognized Miss Manning

" Miss Manning ! " he exclaimed, in surprise. " How do you happen to be here?"

"I came to see you, Rufus."

"Has anything happened?" he asked anxiously, seeing the troubled expression of her countenance. "Nothing is the matter with Rose, is there?"

"She has gone."

"Gone!"

"Yes, she has disappeared."

"Don't say that, Miss Manning. Tell me quick all about it."

"I sent her out on an errand this morning, just around the corner, for a spool of cotton, and she has not got back."

"Do you think she lost her way?"

"She couldn't very well do that, it was so near by. No, Rufus, I am afraid she has been carried off by your stepfather."

"What makes you think so, Miss Manning?" demanded Rufus, in excitement.

"I waited half an hour after she went out, wondering what could keep her so long. Then I began to feel anxious, and put on my bonnet, and slipped downstairs into the street. I went round to the store, and found she had gone there and made the purchase, and gone away directly. I was wondering what to do next, when one of the neighbors came up, and said she saw Rose dragged away by a tall man. She gave me a description of him, and it corresponds exactly to the description of Mr. Martin. I am afraid, Rufus, that he has carried our dear little Rose away. What shall we do?"

"I'll have her back," said Rufus, energetically. "He's got her now; but he shan't keep her. But I'm afraid," he added, sorrowfully, "she'll be ill treated before I can recover her, poor Rose!"

12

CHAPTER XVI.

HOW ROSE FARED.

WE return to Rose, who found herself very unwillingly once more in the custody of her stepfather.

" Go out and play in the back yard with Fanny,"
said Mrs. Waters. " You'll have a nice time together, and be good friends in less than no time."

Rose followed Fanny slowly into the back yard ;
but she had very little hope of a good time. She
was too full of sorrowful thoughts for that. As she
looked back, a moment after going into the yard, she
saw Mr. Martin shaking his fist at her from the back
window, and this she understood very well was a
sign of the treatment which she had to expect.

The back yard was not a very pleasant place. It
was very small to begin with, and the little space
was littered with broken bottles and rubbish of vari
ous kinds. In one corner was a cistern nearly full of
water, which had been standing long enough to be
come turbid.

"What shall we do?" asked Fanny.

"I don't know," said Rose, without much interest

"I'll tell you," said Fanny, "we'll take a piece of wood, and sail it in the cistern. We **can** make be lieve it's a ship."

"You can do it," said Rose.

"Won't you play too?"

"I don't feel much like playing."

"Why don't you?" asked Fanny, **curiously.**

"I wish I was back in New York."

"Who were you with?"

"With Rufie."

"Who's he?"

"My brother."

"Is he a nice boy?"

"Yes, he's the nicest boy that ever **lived**," said Rose, positively.

"Your father says he's a bad boy."

"He isn't my father."

"Isn't your father?"

"No, he's only my stepfather."

Rose was about to say something against Mr. Martin; but it occurred to her that if it came to the ears of the latter, she might fare the worse for it, and accordingly she stopped short.

Fanny picked up a stick, and began to sail it about in the cistern. After a while Rose went up, and looked on rather listlessly. At length Fanny got tired of this amusement, and began to look around for something better to do. In the corner of the yard she spied the cat, who was lying down in a lazy attitude, purring contentedly as she dozed.

"I know what I'll do," she said; "I'll have some fun with puss."

She lifted the sleepy cat, and conveyed her straightway to the cistern. This attracted the attention of Rose, who exclaimed, "What are you going to do?"

"I am going to see puss swim," said the mischievous girl.

Now Rose had a tender heart, and could not bear to see an animal abused. It always aroused all the chivalry in her nature, and her indignation in the present case overcame not only her timidity, but the depression she had felt at the separation from her friends.

"You shan't do it," she said, energetically,

"Mind your business!" said Fanny, defiantly, "It's my cat, and I'm going to put her into the vater."

True to her declaration, she dropped the cat into the cistern.

Rose waited for no more, but ran to the cistern, and, pushing Fanny forcibly away, seized the cat by her neck, and pulled her out.   Puss, on being rescued, immediately took to her heels, and soon was out of harm's way.

"What did you do that for?" exclaimed Fanny, flaming with rage.

"You had no right to put the cat in the water," retorted Rose, intrepidly.

"I'll put you in the water," said Fanny. "I wish you were drowned."

"You're a bad girl," said Rose.

"I won't play with you."

"I don't want you to. I don't care about playing with a girl that behaves so."

"I behave as well as you do, anyway."

"I don't want to talk to you any more."

This seemed to exasperate Fanny, who, overcome
by her feelings, flew at Rose, and scratched her in
the face. Rose was very peaceably inclined, but she
did not care about submitting to such treatment.
She therefore seized Fanny by the hands and hel
them. Unable to get away, Fanny screamed at the
top of her voice. This brought her mother to the
door.   .

"What's going on here?" she asked, in a voice of
authority.

"She's fighting me," said Fanny. "Take her
away."

"Let go my child at once, you wicked girl!" said
Mrs. Waters, whose sympathies were at once enlisted
on the side of her child.

"Then she mustn't scratch me," said Rose.

"What did you scratch her for, Fanny?"

"She's been plaguing me."

"How did she plague you?"

"I was playing with puss, and she came and took
the cat away, and pushed me."

"You are a bad, quarrelsome girl," said Mrs. Wa
ters, addressing Rose, "and I'm sorry I told your fa

ther you might come here. He told me you were bad;
but I didn't think you would show out so quick. If
you were my girl, I'd give you a good whipping.
As it is, I shall inform your father of your conduct,
as soon as he gets home, and I have no doubt he
will punish you."

"I only tried to prevent Fanny from drowning the
cat," said Rose. "She threw her into the water,
and I took her out."

"That's a likely story. I don't believe it. Is it
true, Fanny?"

"No, it isn't," said Fanny, whose regard for truth
was not very strong.

"So I supposed. You have not only ill-treated
my girl, but you have told a wrong story besides.
Fanny, come in, and I will give you a piece of cake."

"You won't give her any, will you, ma?"

"No, she don't deserve any."

With a look of triumph Fanny went into the house,
leaving poor Rose to meditate in sorrow upon this
new phase of injustice and unhappiness. It seemed
as if everybody was conspiring to injure and ill-treat
her.

"I wish Rufie were here," she said, "so that he might take me away."

Then came to her mind the threat of her step-father, and she shuddered at the idea of Rufus being killed. From what she knew of Mr. Martin, she didn't think it very improbable that he would carry out his threat.

After a while she was called to dinner, but she had very little appetite.

"So you're sullen, are you, miss?" said Mrs. Waters. "You're a bad girl, and if I were your father, I'd give you a lesson. So you won't eat!"

"I am not hungry," said Rose.

"I understand very well what that means. However, if you don't want to eat, I won't make you. You'll be hungry enough by and by, I guess."

The afternoon passed very dismally to poor Rose. Fanny was forbidden by her mother to play with her, though this Rose didn't feel at all as a privation She was glad to be free from the company of the little girl whom she had begun to dislike, and spent her time in brooding over her sorrowful fate. She sat by the window, and looked at the people passing by, but she took little interest in the sight, and was in that unhappy state when the future seems to contain nothing pleasant.

At length Mr. Martin came home. His nose was as radiant as ever, and there was little doubt that he had celebrated his capture in the manner most agreeable to him.

" So you're here, are you?" he said. " I thought you wouldn't run away after what I told you. It'll be a bad day for you and your rascal of a brother if you do. What have you been doing?"

" Sitting by the window."

" Where's the other little girl? Why don't you go and play with her, instead of moping here?"

" I don't like her," said Rose.

" 'Pears to me you're mighty particular about your company," said Martin. " Maybe she don't like you any better."

To this Rose didn't reply; but Mrs. Waters, who just then chanced to enter the room, did.

" Your little girl abused my Fanny," she said; " and I had to forbid them playing together. I found them fighting together out in the back yard."

"It wasn't my fault," said Rose.

"Don't tell me that," said Martin. "I know you of old, miss. You're a troublesome lot, you and your brother; but now I've got you back again, I mean to tame you; see if I don't."

"I hope you will," said Mrs. Waters; "my Fanny is a very sweet-dispositioned child, just like what I was at her age; and she never gets into no trouble with nobody, unless they begin to pick on her, and then she can't be expected to stand still, and be abused."

"Of course not," said Martin.

"Your little girl attacked her, and tried to stop her playing with the cat."

"What did you do that for, miss?" said Mr. Martin, menacingly.

"She threw the cat into the cistern," said Rose; "and I was afraid she would drown."

"What business was it of yours? It wasn't your cat, was it?"

"No."

"It was my daughter's cat," said Mrs. Waters; "but she tells me she didn't throw her into the cisʍʌn. It's my belief that your little girl did it her⸱ self."

"Just as likely as not," said Martin, with a hic cough. "Hark you, miss," he continued, steadying himself by the table on which he rested his hand, for his head was not altogether steady, "I've got some‑ thing to say to you, and you'd better mind what I say. Do you hear?"

Rose didn't answer.

"Do you hear, I say?" he demanded, in a louder tone, frowning at the child.

"Yes."

"You'd better, then, just attend to your own busı ness, for you'll find it best for yourself. You've begun to cut up your shines pretty early. But you don't do it while I'm here. What are you snivelling about?"—for Rose, unable to repress her sorrow, began to sob. "What are you snivelling about, I say?"

"I want to go back, and live with Rufie and Miss Manning," said Rose. "Oh, do let me go!"

"That's a pretty cool request," said Martin.

"After I've been so long hunting you up, you expect me to let you go as soon as I've got you. I don't mean to let you go back to Rufie," he said, mimick ing the little girl's tone, — "not if I know it. Be sides," he added, with a sudden thought, "I couldn' do it very well if I wanted to. Do you know where your precious brother is?"

"Where?" asked Rose, in alarm.

"Over to Blackwell's Island. He was took up this morning for stealing."

"I don't believe it," said Rose, indignantly. "I know he wouldn't steal."

"Oh, well, have it your own way, then. Perhaps you know better than I do. Only I'm glad I'm not where he is."

Of course this story was all a fabrication, invented to tease poor Rose. Though the little girl didn't believe it, she feared that Rufus might have got into some trouble, — some innocent persons are sometimes unjustly suspected, — and the bare possibility of such a thing was sufficient to make her feel unhappy. · Poor child! But yesterday she had been full of innocent

joy and happiness, and now everything seemed dark
and sorrowful. When should she see Rufie again?
That was the anxious thought that kept her awake
half the night.

CHAPTER XVII

SEARCHING FOR ROSE.

If Rose passed an unhappy afternoon and evening at the new home in Brooklyn, her brother was scarcely less unhappy in his old home in New York. He loved his little sister devotedly, and the thought that she might be receiving ill-treatment troubled him exceedingly. But there was this difference between them: Rose was timid, and saw no other way but to endure whatever hardships her lot imposed upon her. Rough and Ready, on the other hand, was bold and enterprising, and not easily discouraged. His first thought, therefore, was to get his sister back again. He had never been afraid of his stepfather for himself, only for his mother, while she lived, and afterwards for his little sister. In the present case, he knew that Martin was irritated at his withdrawing the little girl from him, and feared that she would fare the worse now on this account.

He spent the evening with Miss Manning, who was scarcely less troubled than himself at the loss of Rose. The lonely seamstress had found a great solace and comfort in the society of the little girl, and her heart had been drawn to her. She missed her sweet face, and the thousand questions which Rose was in the habit of asking as they sat together through the long day, which didn't seem half so long now as formerly, when she was alone.

When Rufus entered the little room, the first object his eyes rested upon was the little reading-book from which Rose had been in the habit of getting her daily lessons. "When will she read in it again?" he thought, with a pang.

"She was getting along so well in her reading," said Miss Manning, who divined his thoughts. "It's such a pity she should be taken away just at this time."

"I'll have her back, Miss Manning, you may depend upon it," said Rufus, energetically. "If she's anywhere in the city I'll find her."

"The city is a large place, Rufus," said the seamstress, a little despondently.

"That's true, but I shan't have to look all over it. Mr. Martin isn't very likely to be found in Fifth Avenue, unless he's better off than he used to be. He's somewhere in the lower part of the city, on the east side, and that's where I'll look. 'Twouldn't be much use lookin' over the arrivals at the Astor House, or St. Nicholas."

"That's true," said Miss Manning, smiling faintly

There was reason in what the newsboy said; but, as we know, he was mistaken in one point, — Mr. Martin was not in the lower part of the city, on the east side, but in Brooklyn, but it was only the accident of his having found work there, which had caused him to remove across the river.

"Where shall you look first?" asked Miss Manning.

"I shall go to Leonard Street, where we used to live."

"Do you think your stepfather lives there now?"

"No; but perhaps I can find out there where he does live."

Rufus went round to the Lodging House at the usual time. On getting up in the morning, instead of going to the paper offices as usual, he went round to Leonard Street. His anxiety to gain, if possible, some tidings about Rose would not permit him to delay unnecessarily.

Just in front of his old home he saw a slatternly looking woman, one of the inmates of the tenement house. She recognized the newsboy at once.

"Where did you come from?" she asked. "I haven't seen you for a long time."

"No, I'm living in another place now. Have you seen anything of Mr. Martin, lately?"

"Aint you living with him now?"

"No, I've left him. I suppose he isn't in the old room."

"No, he went away some weeks ago. The agent was awful mad because he lost his rent."

"Then he hasn't been back since?"

"I haven't seen him. Maybe some of the rest in the house may know where he is. Are you going to live with him again?"

"No," said the newsboy; "I'd rather take care of myself."

"And how's that little sister of yours?"

13

" He's carried her off. That's why I'm tryin' to find him. If it wasn't for that I wouldn't trouble myself."

" You don't say so? Well, that's a pity. He isn't fit to take care of her. I hope you'll find her."

" Thank you, Mrs. Simpson. I guess I'll go up-stairs and ask some of the rest."

Rough and Ready ascended the stairs, and called upon some of his old acquaintances, with inquiries of a similar character. But he got no. information likely to be of service to him. Martin had not been seen near his old lodgings since the day when he had disappeared, leaving his rent unpaid.

" Where shall I go next?" thought the newsboy, irresolutely.

This was a question more easily asked than answered. He realized that to seek for Rose in the great city, among many thousands of houses, was something like seeking a needle in a haystack.

" I'll go and get my papers," he decided, " and while I am selling them, perhaps I may think of where to go next. It'll be a hard job; but I'm bound to find Rose if she's in the city."

That she was in the city he did not entertain a

doubt. Otherwise, he might have felt less sanguine of ultimate success.

He obtained his usual supply of papers, and going to his wonted stand began to ply his trade.

" You're late this morning, aint you?" asked **Ben** Gibson, a boot-black, who generally stood at the cor- ner of Nassau Street and Printing-House Square " Overslept yourself, didn't you?"

" No," said the newsboy ; " but I had an errand to do before I began."

" Get paid for it?"

" Not unless I pay myself. It was an errand of my own."

" I can't afford to work for myself," said Ben. " A chap asked me, yesterday, why I didn't black my own shoes. I axed him who was to pay me for doin' it. Blackin' costs money, and I can't afford to work for nothin'."

Ben's shoes certainly looked as if no blacking had ever been permitted to soil their virgin purity. Indeed, it is rather a remarkable circumstance that though the boot-blacks generally have at least three-fourths of their time unoccupied, and sometimes remain idle for hours at a time, it never occurs to them (so far, at least, as the writer's observation extends) to use a little of their time and blacking in improving the condition of their own shoes or boots, when they hap pen to have any. Whether this is owing to a spirit of economy, or to the same cause which hinders a phy sician from swallowing his own pills, it is not easy to say. The newsboys, on the contrary, occasionally indulge in the luxury of clean shoes.

"Your shoes don't look as if they'd been blacked lately," said Rough and Ready.

"No more they haven't. They can't stand such rough treatment. It would be too much for their del- icate constitutions."

This was not improbable, since the shoes in ques- tion appeared to be on their last legs, if such an ex- pression may be allowed.

"I like to have my shoes look neat," said Rufus.

"Don't you want a shine?" asked Ben, with a professional air.

"Can't afford it. Maybe I will, though, if you'll trade."

"As how?"

" Shine my shoes, and I'll give you a ' Sun.' "

" That aint but two cents," said Ben, dubiously.

" I know that ; but you oughtn't to charge me more than the wholesale price."

" Anything in the ' Sun ' this mornin' ? "

" Full account of a great murder out in Buffalo," said the newsboy, in his professional tone.

" Well, I don't know but I'll do it," said Ben. " Only if a gent comes along what wants a shine, you must let me off long enough to do the job I'll finish yours afterwards."

" All right."

Ben got out his brush, and, getting on his knees, began operations.

" ' Herald,' ' Times,' ' Tribune,' ' World ! ' " the newsboy continued to cry.

" Seems to me, young man, you're rather particular about your appearance for a newsboy," said a gentleman, who came up just as Ben was giving the finishing touch to the first shoe.

" Oh," said Ben, speaking for his customer, " he only sells papers for amoosement. He's a young chap of fortune, and is first cousin to the King of Mulberry Street.

"Indeed! I think I must purchase a paper then. You may give me the 'Herald.'"

"Here it is, sir."

"Do you also black boots for amusement?" addressing Ben.

"Well," said Ben, "it may be a very amoosin' occupation for some, but I find it rather wearin' to the knees of my pantaloons. It sort of unfits me for genteel society."

"Then why don't you select some other business?"

"'Cause I can't make up my mind whether I'd rather be a lawyer or a banker. While I'm decidin' I may as well black boots."

"You're an original, I see."

"Thank you for the compliment;" and Ben rose from his knees, having made the newsboy's second shoe shine like a mirror. "Now, mister, if you'd like to have your boots shined up by a gentleman in reduced circumstances, I'm ready for the job."

" Well, perhaps I may as well. So you're in reduced circumstances, my lad ? "

" Yes, sir ; my aristocratic relatives have disowned me since I took to blackin' boots, just like they did Ferdinand Montressor, in the great play at the Old Bowery, when he lost his fortun' and went to tend ing bar for a livin'."

" I suppose Ferdinand came out right in the end, didn't he ? "

" Yes, sir ; owing to the death of fifteen of his nearest relations, who got blown up in a steamboat explosion, he became the owner of Montressor Castle, and a big pile of money besides, and lived happy forever after."

" Well, my lad, perhaps you'll be lucky too."

" Maybe you're meanin' to give me a quarter for blackin' your boots," said Ben, shrewdly.

" No, I wasn't intending to do it ; but, as you're a gentleman in reduced circumstances, I don't know but I will."

" Thank you, sir," said Ben, pocketing the money with satisfaction. " Any time you want your boots

blacked, just call on me, and I'll give you the bulli-
est shine you ever saw."

"All right, good-morning!   When you get into
your castle, I'll come and see you."

"Thank you, sir.   I hope you'll live long enough
to do it."

"That's wishing me a long life, I take it," said the
gentleman, smiling.

"You're in luck, Ben," said the newsboy.

"That's so.   He's what I call a gentleman."

"Lucky for you he isn't in reduced circumstances
like me.   Here's your 'Sun.'   When I get rich I'll
pay you better."

Ben began to spell out the news in the 'Sun,' with
some difficulty, for his education was limited, and
Rufus continued to cry his papers.

At the end of half an hour, happening to have his
face turned towards the corner of Nassau Street, he
made a sudden start as he saw the familiar figure of
Martin, his stepfather, just turning into the Square.

CHAPTER XVIII.

A PARLEY WITH THE ENEMY.

IT has already been stated that James Martin's motive in recovering Rose was not a feeling of affection for her, for this he had never had, but rather a desire to thwart Rufus in his plans. The newsboy's refusal to work for his support had incensed his stepfather, and Martin was a man who was willing to take considerable trouble to gratify his spite.

It was quite in accordance with this disposition of his, that, after recovering Rose in the manner we have seen, he was not content, until he had seen her brother, and exulted over him. On the day succeeding, therefore, instead of going to work, he came over to New York, for the express purpose of witnessing our hero's grief and chagrin at the loss of his sister. He knew very well where to find him.

Rough and Ready surveyed the approach of his

stepfather with mingled anger and anxiety   He it was that held in his power the one whom the news-boy loved best.   Rufus guessed his motive in seeking him now, and, knowing that he intended to speak to him, awaited his address in silence.

"Well, Rufus," said Mr. Martin, with a malicious grin, "how are you this morning?"

"I am well," said the newsboy, shortly.

"I am glad to hear it," said Martin; "I'd ought to feel glad of it, you've been such a dootiful son."

"I am not your son," said Rough and Ready, in a tone which indicated that he was very glad that no such relationship existed between them.

"That's lucky for me," said Martin; "I wouldn't own such a young cub.   When I have a son, I hope he'll be more dootiful, and treat me with more grati-tude."

"What should I be grateful for?" demanded the newsboy, quickly.

"Didn't I take care of you, and give you victuals and clothes for years?"

"Not that I know of," said Rufus, coolly.   "I've

had to support myself, and help support you, ever since we came to New York."

"So you complain of having to work, do you? 'Cause I was a poor man, and couldn't support you in idleness, you think you're ill used."

"I never complained of having to work. I am willing to work hard for myself — and Rose."

"How is Rose now? I hope she is well," said Martin, with a smile of triumph.

"That's what I'd like to have you tell me," said Rufus, looking steadily at Martin. "Where have you carried my sister?"

"What should I know of your sister?" said Martin. "The last I knew, you kidnapped her from my care and protection."

"Your care and protection!" repeated Rough and Ready, disdainfully. "What care did you ever take of her? You did nothing for her support, but came home drunk about every day. You couldn't take care of yourself, much less any one else."

"Do you want a licking?" asked Martin, angrily, approaching a little nearer.

Rough and Ready didn't budge an inch, for he was
not in the least afraid of his stepfather.

"I wouldn't advise you to try it, Mr. Martin," he
said, composedly. "I am able to take care of myself."

"Are you? I am happy to hear it," sneered Martin, repressing his anger, as he thought that, after all,
he had it in his power to punish Rufus more effect-
ually and safely through his sister than by any
attempt at present violence. "I'm happy to hear it,
for I've relieved you of any other care. I will take
care of Rose now."

"Where is she?" asked Rufus, anxiously.

"She's safe," said Martin.

"Is that all you are going to tell me?"

"It's all you need to know. Only, if you're very
anxious to contribute to your sister's support, you
can hand me the money, and it shall go for her
board."

As he looked at Martin with his air of insolent
triumph, the newsboy felt that he hated him. It was
not a Christian feeling, but it was a very natural
one. This was the man who had made his mother's

life a wretched one, and hastened her death ; who ir this and other ways had brought grief and trouble upon Rose and himself, and who now seemed determined to continue his persecutions, out of a spirit of miserable spite and hatred. He would hardly have been able to control his temper, but he knew that Martin would probably wreak vengeance upon his sister for anything he might do to provoke him, and he resolved, poor as the chance was, to try and see if he could not conciliate him, and induce him, if possible, to give up Rose again to his own care.

"Mr. Martin," he said, "Rose will only be a trouble and expense to you. Why won't you bring her back? You don't care for her; but she is my sister, and I will willingly work for her support."

"Rose must stay with me," said Martin. "If you're so anxious to pay her expenses, you can pay me."

"I want her to live with me."

"Sorry I couldn't accommodate you," said Martin, "but your influence was bad on her. I can't allow you to be together. She's been growing a great deal wus since she was with me. I carried her yesterday

to a nice, respectable boarding-place, and the fust
thing she did was to get to fighting with another
little gal in the house."

" Where was that? "

" Maybe you'd like to have me tell you."

" Rose is a very sweet, peaceable little girl, and if
she got into trouble, the other girl was to blame."

" The other girl's a little angel, so her mother
says, and she ought to know.   Rose has got a sullen,
bad temper ; but I'll break her of it, see if I don't."

" If you ill-treat my sister, it'll be the worse for
you," said Rough and Ready, hotly.

" Hoity-toity, I guess I can punish my child, if I
see fit, without asking your leave."

" She isn't your child."

" I've got her in my charge, and I mean to keep
her."

This was unfortunately true, and Rufus chafed in-
wardly that it was so.   To think that his darling
little Rose should be in the power of such a coarse
brute was enough to fill him with anger and despair.
But what could he do?   Was there any way in which
he could get her back?   If he only knew where she

was! But of this he was entirely ignorant. Indignant as he was, he must use conciliating means as long as there was any chance that these would avail anything. He thought of the money he had laid aside, and it occurred to him that Mr. Martin might be accessible to a bribe. He knew that his stepfather was very poorly provided with money, unless he had greatly improved in his habits upon his former mode of life. At all events, he could but fail, and he determined to make the attempt.

"Mr. Martin," he said, "if you'll bring my sister back, and agree not to take her away from me again, I'll give you ten dollars."

"Have you got so much money?" asked Martin, doubtfully.

"Yes."

"Where did you get it?"

"I earned it."

"Have you got any more?"

"A little."

The newsboy did not think it expedient to let his stepfather know precisely how much he had, for he knew his demands would rise with the knowledge.

" How much more?" persisted Martin.

" I can't exactly say."

" Have you got fifteen dollars?"

" I will try to raise it, if you will bring back my sister."

Martin hesitated. Fifteen dollars was not to be despised. This sum would enable him to live in idleness for a time. Besides he would be relieved of the expenses of Rose, and this would amount in time to considerable. As he did not pretend to feel any attachment to his stepdaughter, and didn't expect to receive any pleasure or comfort from her society, it certainly seemed to be a desirable arrangement. But, on the other hand, it was pleasant to a man like Martin to feel that he had some one in his power over whom he could exercise control, and upon whom he might expend his anger. Besides, he would keep Rufus in a constant state of trouble and anxiety, and this, too, was something. Still he did not like to give up wholly the chance of gaining the fifteen dollars. After a little hesitation, he said, " Have you got the money with you?"

" No."

" Have you any of it with you ? "

" Only a dollar or two."

" That won't do."

" Why do you ask ? "

" Because I should want part or the whole of it in advance."

" I shouldn't be willing to pay you in advance," said the newsboy, whose confidence in his stepfather's integrity was by no means large.

" Why not ? "

" I'll pay you when you bring Rose. That's fair enough."

" Perhaps you wouldn't have the money."

" Then you could carry her back again."

" And have all my trouble for nothing ! "

" You won't have all your trouble for nothing. I want Rose back, and I shall be sure to have the money with me."

Mr. Martin reflected a moment. He knew that he could trust the newsboy's word. Much as he disliked him, he knew that if he made a promise he would keep it, if there was a possibility of his doing so. Fifteen dollars was quite a sum to him, for it was a

14

iong time since he had had so much, and such were
his shiftless habits, that it would probably be a long
time before he would have it, especially if he had to
pay for the board of Rose.   Again, it occurred to him
that if he should surrender Rose, and receive the
money, he might steal her again, and thus lose noth
ing.   But then it was probable that Rufus would
guard against this by removing to a different quarter
of the city, and not permitting Rose to go out unac
companied.

So there was a little conflict in his mind, and
finally he came to this decision.   He would not sur
render Rose quite yet.   He wanted to torment both
her and her brother a little longer.   There was time
enough to make the arrangement a week hence.   Perhaps by that time the newsboy would be ready to
increase his offer.

" Well," said Rough and Ready, " what do **you**
say ? "

" I'll think about it."

" You'd better decide now."

" No, I don't feel like it.   Do you think I'm ready
to give up my little daughter's society, after having

her with me only a day?" and he smiled in a way that provoked Rufus, as he knew it would.

" Will you bring her to-morrow?" asked the news boy, who felt that he must hold his anger in check.

" Maybe I'll bring her in the course of a week ; that is, if she behaves herself. I must break her of some of her faults. She needs trainin'."

" She's a good little girl."

" She's got to be better before I give her back. Hope you won't fret about her ; " and Martin walked away, with a half laugh, as he saw the trouble which the newsboy couldn't help showing in his face.

A sudden idea came to Rufus.

" Ben," he said, beckoning to Ben Gibson, who had just got through with a job, " do you see that man?"

" The one you've been talking with?"

" Yes."

" Well, what about him?"

" I'll give you a dollar if you'll follow him, and find out where he lives. Of course he mustn't know that you are following him."

" Maybe he isn't going home."

" Never mind. Follow him if it takes you all **day,** and you shall have the dollar."

" Maybe I'll get off the track."

" You're too sharp for that. You see, Ben, he's carried off my little sister, and I want to find out where he has put her. Just find out for me where she is, and we'll carry her off from him."

" That'll be bully fun," said Ben. " I'm your man. Just take care of my box, and I'll see what I can do."

Mr. Martin had turned down Spruce Street. He kept on his way, not suspecting that there was some one on his track.

CHAPTER XIX.

ROSE AGAIN IN TROUBLE.

LEAVING Ben Gibson on the track of Mr. Martin, we must return to Rose, and inquire how she fared in her new home at Brooklyn. Mrs. Waters had already taken a strong prejudice against her, on account of the misrepresentations of her daughter Fanny. If Fanny was an angel, as her mother represented, then angels must be very disagreeable people to live with. The little girl was rude, selfish, and had a violent temper. Had Mr. Martin stood by Rose, her treatment would have been much better, for policy would have led Mrs. Waters to treat her with distinguished consideration; but as parental fondness was not a weakness of her stepfather, the boarding-house keeper felt under no restraint.

"What shall I do if your little girl behaves badly, Mr. Martin?" said Mrs. Waters, as he was about to leave the house in the morning.

" Punish her, ma'am. You needn't feel no deli:acy about it. I'll stand by you. She's a bad, trouble-some girl, and a good whipping every day is just what she needs. Do you hear that, miss?"

Rose did not answer, but her lip quivered a little. It seemed hard to the little girl, fresh from the atmos-phere of love by which she had been surrounded in her recent home, to be treated with such injustice and unfairness.

" Why don't you answer, miss?" roai̇d James Martin, savagely. " Didn't you hear whal I said?"

" Yes," said Rose.

" Mind you remember it, then. If you don't be-have yourself, Mrs. Waters has my full peimission to punish you, and if she don't punish you enough, I'll give you a little extra when I get home. I shall ask her to report to me about you. Do you hear?"

" Yes."

" Yes! Where's your manners? Say 'Yes, sir.'"

" Yes, sir."

" Mind you remember then. And there's one thing more. Don't you go to run away. If you do, it'll be the worse for your brother."

With this parting threat he went out of the house.

"Now, children," said Mrs. Waters, "go out and play. I'm up to my elbows in work, and I can't have you in the way."

"Where shall we go?" asked Rose.

" Out in the back yard."

"I don't want to go out in the back yard," said Fanny; "there aint anything to do there."

" Well, go out into the street then, if you want to."

"Yes, I'd rather go there."

Rose followed Fanny into the street in rather a listless manner, for she did not expect much enjoyment.

" Now, what shall we do?" asked Fanny.

" I don't know, I'm sure," said Rose.

" I know where there's a candy-shop."

"Do you?"

" Yes, just at the corner. Do you like candy?"

" Yes, pretty well."

"You haven't got any money, have you?" said Fanny, insinuatingly.

" No, I haven't," answered Rose.

" I wish you had. I like candy, but mother won't give me any money to buy any. She's real mean."

" Do you call your mother mean?" said Rose, rather shocked.

" Yes, she might give me a penny. Oh, there's a hand-organ. Come, let's go and hear it."

An Italian, with a hand-organ, had taken his station before a house in the next block. There was a half-grown girl with a tambourine in his company, and, best of all, a monkey was perched on the performer's shoulder, with his tail curled up in a ring, and his head covered with a red cap, and his sharp little eyes roving from one to another of the motley group drawn around the organ, keenly watching for the stray pennies which were bestowed as much for the sake of seeing the monkey pick them up, as a compensation for the music, which was of rather an inferior order, even for a hand-organ.

" Let's go and hear the organ," repeated Fanny.

To this proposal Rose made no objection. Children are not critical in music, and the tunes which issued from the wheezy organ had their attraction for her. The monkey was equally attractive with his

queer, brown face, and Rose was very willing to go
nearer with her companion.

"Aint he a funny monkey?" said Fanny. "He
took off his hat to me. I wish I had a penny to
throw to him, though I don't think I'd give it to him.
I'd rather spend it for candy," she added, after a little reflection.

Here the organ struck up "Old Dog Tray," that
veteran melody, which celebrates, in rather doleful
measure, the fidelity and kindness of its canine hero.
But the small crowd of listeners were not apprecia
tive, as in response to the strains only a solitary
penny was forthcoming, and this was thrown by a
butcher's boy, who chanced to be passing. The
Italian, concluding probably that he was not likely
to realize a fortune in that locality, shouldered his
hand-organ, and moved up the street.

"Let's go after him," said Fanny.

"Shall you know the way back?" said Rose.

"Yes, I know well enough," said Fanny, carelessly.

Rose accordingly followed her without hesitation,
and when the Italian again stopped, the two little

girls made a part of his audience.   After going through his series of tunes, and gathering a small stock of pennies, the organ-grinder again started on his travels.   Rose and Fanny, having no better amusement before them, still kept his company, and this continued for an hour or two.

By this time they had unconsciously got a consid erable distance from home.   There is no knowing how far they would have gone, had not the tambou rine player detected Fanny in picking up a penny which had been thrown for the musicians.   Fanny, supposing that she was not observed, slipped it into her pocket slily, intending to spend it for candy on her way home.   But she was considerably alarmed when the girl, her dark face full of indignation, ran forward, and, seizing her by the arm, shook her, uttering the while an incoherent medley of Italian and English.

" What's the row?   What has the little girl done?" asked a man in the group.

" She one tief.   She took penny, and put in her pocket," said the Italian girl, continuing to shake her.

Fanny protested with tears that she had not done it, but a boy near by testified that he had seen her do it. With shame and mortification, Fanny was obliged to produce the purloined penny, and give it to the monkey, who, in spite of her intended dishonesty, had the politeness to remove his hat, and make her a very ceremonious bow.

"I should think you'd be ashamed of yourselves," said a stout woman, addressing both little girls.

"I didn't take the penny," said Rose, resenting the imputation ; "I wouldn't steal for anything."

"She wanted me to take it," said Fanny, maliciously, "so that I could buy some candy for her."

"That's a story," said Rose, indignantly ; "I didn't know you meant to do it, till I saw you slip it into your pocket."

"I've no doubt one's as bad as the other," said the woman, with commendable inpartiality.

"Go 'way," said the tambourine girl ; "you steal some more penny."

"Come away, Fanny," said Rose ; "I'm ashamed to stay here any longer, and I should think you would be."

As circumstances made the neighborhood of the musicians rather unpleasant, Fanny condescended to adopt the suggestion of her companion.

" I guess I'll go home," she said. " I'm hungry, and ma'll give me some gingerbread. She won't give you any, for you're a bad girl."

" What are you?" retorted Rose.

'' I'm a good girl.'"

" I never heard of a good girl's stealing," said Rose.

" If you say that again, I'll strike you," said Fanny, who was rather sensitive about the charge, particularly as it happened to be true.

Rose was not fond of disputing, and made no reply, but waited for Fanny to show her the way home. But this Fanny was unable to do. She had followed the organ-grinder round so many corners that she had quite lost her reckoning, and had no idea where she was. She stood undecided, and looked helplessly around her.

" I don't know where to go," she said.

" Don't you know the way home?" asked Rose.

" No," answered Fanny, almost ready to cry.

Rose hardly knew whether to be glad or to be sorry. If she should be lost, and not find her way back to the boarding-house, there would be this comfort at least, that she would be separated from Mr. Martin. Still she was not quite prepared to live in the streets, and didn't know how to go to work to find her brother. Besides, Mr. Martin had threatened to harm him in case she ran away. So, on the whole, she was rather in hopes that Fanny would remember the way.

"We'd better go straight along," suggested Rose, "and perhaps we shall find your house."

As Fanny had no better plan to propose, they determined to adopt this plan. Neither had taken any particular notice of the way by which they had come, and were therefore unable to recognize any landmarks. So, instead of nearing home, they were actually getting farther and farther away from it, and there is no knowing where they would finally have brought up, if in turning a corner they had not found themselves all at once face to face with Mrs. Waters herself. It may be explained that the latter, after an hour, not hearing the voices of the children outside, had become alarmed, and started in pursuit. She had already had a long and weary walk, and it was only by the merest chance that she caught sight of them. This long walk, with the anxiety which she had felt, had not improved her temper, but made her angry, so that she was eager to vent her indignation upon the two children.

"What do you mean, you little plagues, by run ning away?" she asked, seizing each child roughly by the arm. "Here I've been rushing round the streets after you, neglecting my work, for a good hour."

"She wanted to go," said Fanny, pointing to Rose.

"So she led you away, did she?" asked Mrs. Waters, giving Rose a rough shake.

"Yes, she wanted me to go after an organ," said Fanny, seeing a way to screen herself at the expense of her companion, and like a mean little coward availing herself of it.

"So this is another one of your tricks, miss, is it?" demanded Mrs. Waters, angrily.

"It isn't true," said Rose. "She asked me to b~."

"Oh, no doubt; you can lie as fast as you can talk," said Mrs. Waters. "I thought all the while that Fanny was too good a girl to give her mother so much trouble. It was only to oblige you that she went off. That comes of having such a bad girl in the family. I shan't keep you long, for you'll be sure to spoil my Fanny, who was one of the best little girls in the neighborhood till you came to lead her into mischief. But I'll come up with you, miss, you may depend upon that. Your father told me I might punish you, and I mean to do it; just wait till we get home, that's all."

Here Mrs. Waters paused more from lack of breath, than because she had given full expression to her feelings. She relaxed her hold upon Fanny, but continued to grasp Rose roughly by the shoulder, dragging her rapidly along.

Rose saw that it was of no use to defend herself. Mrs. Waters was determined to find her guilty, and would not believe any statement she might make.

So she ran along to adapt herself to the pace of the angry woman beside her.

They soon reached the house, and entered, Mrs. Waters pushing Rose before.

"Now for your punishment," said Mrs. Waters, grimly, " I'm going to lock you up down cellar."

"Oh, don't," said Rose, terrified. "I don't want to go down in the dark cellar ; " for, like most children, she had a dread of darkness.

But Mrs. Waters was inexorable. She opened the door of the cellar, and compelled the little girl to descend the dark staircase. Then she slammed the door, and left her sobbing on the lowest step.

Poor Rose! She felt that she had indeed fallen among enemies

CHAPTER XX.

HOW BEN SUCCEEDED.

Ben Gibson was very willing to suspend blacking boots and follow in the track of James Martin, partly because he considered it easier work, but partly also, because he was glad to be of service to the newsboy. The fact was that Rough and Ready was popular among the street boys He was brave and manly, rough with those who tried to impose upon him, but always ready to do a favor to a boy who needed it. Ben had not forgotten how two winters before, when he had been laid up with a sickness brought on by exposure, Rufus had himself contributed liberally to help him, and led other boys to follow his example, thus defraying his expenses until he got about again. A kind heart will make its possessor popular sooner than anything else, and it was this, together with his well-known prowess, which

15

made Rough and Ready not only popular, but admired in the circle to which he belonged.

Ben followed James Martin down Spruce Street, keeping sufficiently in the background, so as not to excite the suspicions of the latter.

"I wonder where he's goin'," thought Ben; "I don't think I could follow him more'n a hundred miles without wantin' to rest. Anyhow I guess I can stand it as well as he can."

Martin walked along in a leisurely manner. The fact was that he had made up his mind not to work that day, and therefore he felt in no particular hurry. This was rather improvident on his part, since he had voluntarily assumed the extra expense of supporting Rose; but then prudence and foresight were not his distinguishing traits. He had a vague idea that the world owed him a living, and that he would rub along somehow or other. This is a mischievous doctrine, and men who deserve to succeed never hold it. It is true, however, that the world is pretty sure to provide a living for those who are willing to work for it, but makes no promises to those who expect to be taken care of without any exertions of their own. The difference between the rich merchant and the ragged fellow who solicits his charity as he is stepping into his carriage, consists, frequently, not in natural ability, but in the fact that the one has used his ability as a stepping-stone to success, and the other has suffered his to become stagnant, through indolence, or dissipation.

But we must come back to Mr. Martin.

He walked down towards the East River till he reached Water Street, then turning to the left, he brought up at a drinking-saloon, which he had vis-ited more than once on a similar errand. He found an old acquaintance who invited him to drink, — an invitation which he accepted promptly.

Ben remained outside.

"I thought he did business at some such place by the looks of his nose," soliloquized Ben. "What shall I do while I'm waitin' for him?"

Looking around him, Ben saw two boys of about his own age pitching pennies. As this was a game with which long practice had made him familiar, he made overtures towards joining them.

"Let a feller in, will you?" he said.

"How much you got?" asked one of the boys, in a business-like way.

"Ten cents," said Ben. "I lent old Vanderbilt most of my money day afore yesterday, to buy up a new railroad, and he haint forked over."

Ben need not have apologized for his comparative poverty, as he proved to be the richest of the three. The game commenced, and continued for some time with various mutations of fortune; but at the end of half an hour Ben found himself richer by two cents than when he had commenced. From time to time he cast a watchful glance at the saloon opposite, for he had no intention of suffering the interest of the game to divert him from the object of his expedition. At length he saw James Martin issue from the saloon, and prepared to follow him.

"Are you going?" asked one of the boys with whom he had been playing.

"Yes, I've got some important business on hand. Here's your money;" and he threw down the two cents he had won.

"You won it?"

"What if I did? I only played for amoosement.

What's two cents to a gentleman of fortune, with a big manshun up town?"

"It's the Tombs, he manes," said one of his late opponents, laughing.

"He can blow, he can," remarked the other.

But Ben couldn't stop to continue the conversation, as James Martin had already turned the corner of the street. It was observable that his gait already showed a slight unsteadiness, which he tried to remedy by walking with unusual erectness. The consequence of this was that he didn't keep fairly in view the occupants of the sidewalk, which led to his deliberately walking into rather a stout female, who was approaching in the opposite direction.

"Is it goin' to murther me ye are, you spalpeen?" she exclaimed, wrathfully, as soon as she could collect her breath. "Don't you know better than to run into a dacent woman in that way?"

"It was you run into me," said Martin, steadying himself with some difficulty after the collision.

"Hear him now," said the woman, looking about her to call attention to the calumny.

"I see how it is," said Martin; "you're drunk, ma'am, you can't walk straight."

This led to a voluble outburst from the irate woman, to which Ben listened with evident enjoyment.

"Am I drunk, boy?" asked Martin, appealing to Ben, whom he for the first time noticed.

"Of course you aint, gov'nor," said Ben. "You never did sich a thing in your life."

"What do you know about it?" demanded the woman. "It's my belief you're drunk yourself."

"Do you know who this gentleman is?" asked Ben, passing over the personal charge.

"No, I don't."

"He's President of the Fifth Avenue Temperance Society," said Ben, impressively. "He's just been drinking the health of his feller-officers in a glass of something stiff, round in Water Street, that's all."

The woman sniffed contemptuously, but, not deigning a reply, passed on.

"Who are you?" asked Martin, turning to Ben. "You're a good feller."

"That's so," said Ben. "That's what everybody says."

"So'm I a good feller," said Martin, whose recent potations must have been of considerable
strength, to judge from their effects. "You know
me."

"Of course I do," said Ben. "I've knowed you
from infancy."

"Take a drink?" said Martin.

"Not at present," said Ben. "My health don't
require it this mornin'."

"Where are you going?"

"Well," said Ben, "I aint very particular. I'm
a wealthy orphan, with nothin' to do. I'll walk along
with you, if it's agreeable."

I wish you would," said Martin; "I aint feeling
quite well this morning. I've got the headache."

"I don't wonder at that," thought Ben. "I'll
accompany you to your residence, if it aint too far
off."

"I live in Brooklyn," said Martin.

"Oho!" thought Ben. "Well, that information
is worth something. Shall we go over Fulton Ferry?" he asked, aloud.

"Yes," said Martin.

"Take hold of my arm, and I'll support your totterin' steps," said Ben.

Mr. Martin, who found locomotion in a straight line rather difficult on account of his headache, willingly availed himself of this obliging offer, and the two proceeded on their way to Fulton Ferry.

"Have you got much of a family?" inquired Ben, by way of being sociable.

"I've got a little girl," said Martin, "and a boy, but he's an impudent young rascal."

"What's his name?"

"Rufus. He sells newspapers in front of the 'Times' office."

"The boys call him Rough and Ready, don't they?"

"Yes. Do you know him?" asked Martin, a little suspiciously. "He aint a friend of yours, is he?"

"I owe him a lickin'," said Ben, with a show of indignation.

"So do I," said Martin. "He's an impudent young rascal."

"So he is," chimed in Ben. "I'll tell you what I'd do, if I were you."

"What?"

"I'd disinherit him. Cut him off with a shillin'."

"I mean to," said Martin, pleased to find sympathy in his dislike to his stepson.

Probably the newsboy would not have suffered acute anguish, had he learned his stepfather's intention to disinherit him, as the well-known lines, "Who steals my purse, steals trash," might at almost any time have been appropriately applied to Mr. Martin's purse, when he happened to carry one.

Ben paid the toll at the ferry, and the two entered the boat together. He conducted Mr. Martin to the Gentleman's Cabin, where he found him a seat in the corner. James Martin sank down, and closed his eyes in a drowsy fit, produced by the liquor he had drunk.

Ben took a seat opposite him.

"You're an interestin' object," soliloquized Ben, as he looked across the cabin at his companion

"It's a great blessin' to be an orphan, if a feller can't own a better father than that. However, I'll stick to him till I get him home. I wonder what he'd say if he knowed what I was goin' with him for. If things don't go contrary, I guess I'll get the little girl away from him afore long."

When the boat struck the Brooklyn pier, James Martin was asleep.

"There aint no hurry," thought Ben; "I'll let him sleep a little while."

After the boat had made three or four trips, Ben went across and shook Martin gently.

The latter opened his eyes, and looked at him vacantly.

"What's the matter?" he said, thickly.

"We've got to Brooklyn," said Ben. "If you want to go home, we'll have to go off the boat."

James Martin rose mechanically, and, walking through the cabin, passed out upon the pier, and then through the gates.

"Where'll we go now?" asked Ben. "Is it far off?"

"Yes, said Martin. "We'll take a horse-car."

" All right, gov'nor; just tell us what one we want, and we'll jump aboard."

Martin was sufficiently in his senses to be able to impart this information correctly. He made no objection to Ben's paying the fare for both, which the latter did, as a matter of policy, thinking that in his present friendly relations with Mr. Martin he was likely to obtain the information he desired, with considerably less difficulty than he anticipated. On the whole, Ben plumed himself on his success, and felt that as a detective he had done very well.

Martin got out at the proper place, and **Ben of** course got out with him.

" That's where I live," said Martin, pointing to the house. " Won't you go in? "

" Thank you for the compliment," said Ben ; " but I've got some important business to attend to, and shall have to be goin'. How's your headache? "

" It's better," said Martin.

" Glad to hear it," said Ben.

Martin, on entering the house, was informed of the ill-conduct of Rose, as Mrs. Waters chose to rep resent it, and that in consequence she had been shut up in the cellar.

"Keep her there as long as you like," said Martin. "She's a bad girl, and it won't do her any harm."

If Rose had known that an agent of her brother's was just outside the house, and was about to carry back to Rufus tidings of her whereabouts, she would have felt considerably better. There is an old saying that the hour which is darkest is just before day.

CHAPTER XXI.

IN AN OYSTER SALOON.

Rough and Ready had just laid in a supply of afternoon papers, and resumed his usual position in front of the " Times " office, when Ben Gibson came round the corner, just returned from his expedition to Brooklyn, the particulars of which are given in the last chapter.

" What luck, Ben?" asked the newsboy, anxiously.

" Tip-top," said Ben.

" You don't mean to say you've found her?" said Rough and Ready, eagerly.

" Yes, I have, — leastways I've found where she's kept."

" Tell me about it.   How did you manage?"

" I followed your respected father down Spruce Street," said Ben.   " He stopped to take a little something strong in Water Street, which made him

rather top-heavy. I offered him my protection, which
he thankfully accepted; so we went home together as
intimate as brothers."

" Did he suspect anything? "

" Not a bit; I told him I know'd you, and owed
you a lickin', which impressed his affectionate heart
very favorably. When'll you take it? "

" What? "

" The lickin'."

" Not at present," said Rough and Ready, laughing. " I guess it'll keep."

" All right. Any time you want it, just let me
know."

" Go ahead. Where does he live? "

" In Brooklyn. We went over Fulton Ferry, and
then took the horse-cars a couple of miles. I paid
the old chap's fare."

" I'll make it right with you. Did you see Rose? "

" No; but I'll remember the house."

" Ben, you're a trump. I was afraid you wouldn't
succeed. Now tell me when I had better go for her?
Shall it be to-night? "

" No," said Ben; " he'll be at home to-night. Be-

sides, she won't be allowed to come out. If we go
over to-morrow, we may meet her walkin' out somewhere. Then we can carry her off without any fuss."

"I don't know but you're right," said the newsboy,
thoughtfully; "but it is hard to wait. I'm afraid she
won't be treated well, poor little Rose!"

Rufus proposed to go over in the evening and re-
connoitre, but it occurred to him that if he were seen
and recognized by Mr. Martin, the latter would be on
his guard, and perhaps remove her elsewhere, or keep
her so strictly guarded that there would be no opportunity of reclaiming her. He was forced, therefore,
to wait with what patience he might till the next
morning. He went round to tell Miss Manning of
his success. She sympathized heartily with him,
for she had felt an anxiety nearly as great as his
own as to the fate of the little girl whose presence
had lighted up her now lonely room with sunshine.

After spending a portion of the evening with her,
he came out again into the streets. It was his usual
time for going to the Lodging House; but he felt
restless and wakeful, and preferred instead to wander
about the streets.

At ten o'clock he felt the promptings of appetite, and, passing an oyster saloon, determined to go in and order a stew.

It was not a very fashionable place. There was a general air of dinginess and lack of neatness pervading the place. The apartment was small, and low-studded. On one side was a bar, on the other, two or three small compartments provided with tables, with curtains screening them from the main room.

It was not a very inviting place, but the newsboy, though more particular than most of his class, reflected that the oysters might nevertheless be good.

"Give us a stew," he said to a young man behind the counter, whose countenance was ornamented with pimples.

"All right. Anything to drink?"

"No sir," said our hero.

Rufus entered the only one of the alcoves which was unoccupied. The curtains of the other two were drawn. The one which he selected was the middle one of three, so that what was going on in both was audible to him. The one in front appeared to have a solitary occupant, and nothing was heard from it but the clatter of a knife and fork.

But there were evidently two persons in the other, for Rufus was able to make out a low conversation which was going on between them. The first words were heard with difficulty, but afterwards, either because they spoke louder or because his ear got more accustomed to the sounds, he made out everything.

" You are sure about the money, Jim," said one.

" Yes."

" How do you know it? "

" Never mind how I know it. It makes no odds as long as he's got it, and we are going to take it."

" That's the main thing. Now tell me your plans."

" He'll be going home about half-past eleven, some-where from there to twelve, and we must lie in wait for him. It's a cool thousand, that'll be five hun-dred apiece."

" I need it bad enough, for I'm dead broke."

" So am I. Got down to my last dollar, and no chance of another, unless this little plan of ours works."

" It's dangerous."

" Of course there's a risk. There won't be any time to lose. The policeman's got a long beat. We must make the attack when he's out of the way. There'll be no time to parley."

" If he resist — "

" Knock him on the head. A minute'll ·be enough."

There was some further conversation carried on in a low voice, from which the newsboy, who listened with attention, gathered full particulars of the meditated attack. It appears that the intended victim of the plot was a Wall Street broker, who was likely to be out late in the evening with a considerable sum of money about him. How the two desperadoes con-cerned in the plot had obtained this information did not appear. This, however, is not necessary to the comprehension of the story. Enough that they had intended to make criminal use of that knowledge.

" What shall I do?" thought the newsboy, when by careful listening he arrived at a full comprehension of the plot in all its details. " There'll be robbery, and perhaps murder done unless I interfere."

It required some courage to do anything. The men were not only his superiors in physical strength, but they were doubtless armed, and ready, if interfered with, to proceed to extremities. But the newsboy had one of those strong and hardy natures to which fear is a stranger, — at least so far as his own safety was concerned. This proceeded from his strength and physical vigor, and entire freedom from that nervousness which often accompanies a more fragile organization.

"I'll stop it if I can," he decided, promptly, without a thought of the risk he might incur.

One circumstance might interfere: they might leave the saloon before he was ready to do so, and thus he would lose track of them. Unfortunately, the place where the attack was to be made had not yet been mentioned. But he was relieved of this apprehension when he heard the curtain drawn aside, and a fresh order given to the waiter. At that moment his own stew was brought, and placed on the table before him.

"I shall get through as soon as they do," thought

Rufus. " There will be nothing to hinder my following them."

After finishing his own oysters, he waited until his
neighbors, who were more deliberate, were ready to go
out. When he heard their departure, he also drew the
curtain, and stepped into the room. He took care not
to look too closely at them, but one quick glance da-
guerreotyped their features in his memory. One was
a short, stout man, with a heavy face and lowering
expression ; the other was taller and slighter, with a
face less repulsive. The former, in rushing into
crime, appeared to be following the instincts of a
brutal nature. The other looked as if he might have
been capable of better things, had circumstances been
different.

The two exchanged a look when they saw the newsboy coming out of the compartment adjoining their
own, as if to inquire whether he was likely to have
heard any of their conversation. But Rufus assumed
such an indifferent and unconcerned an expression,
that their suspicions, if they had any, were dispelled,
and they took no further notice of him.

They settled for what they had eaten, and the

newsboy, hastily throwing down the exact change for his oysters, followed them out.

They turned up a side street, conversing still in a low tone. Rufus, though appearing indifferent, listened intently. At length he heard what he had been anxious to hear, — the scene of the intended attack.

The information gave him this important advantage: He was no longer under the necessity of dogging the steps of the two men, which, if persisted in, would have been likely to attract their attention and arouse their suspicions. He was able now to leave them. All that would be necessary was to be on the spot at the time mentioned, or a little earlier. But what preparations should he make? For a boy to think of engaging single-handed with two ruffians was of course foolhardy. Yet it was desirable that he should have a weapon of some kind. Here, however, there was a difficulty, as there were no shops probably open at that hour, where he could provide himself with what he desired.

While considering with some perplexity what he

should do, he came across Tim Graves, a fellow newsboy, carrying in his hand a bat.

"How are you, Tim?" he said.

"I'm so's to be round. Where are you going?"

"Up-town on an errand. Where'd you get that bat?"

"I was up to the Park to see a base-ball match, and picked it up."

"What'll you take for it?"

"Want to buy?"

"Yes."

"I don't know," said Tim, hesitating. "It's worth a quarter."

"All right. Give it here."

"What do you want it for?"

"Somebody might attack me for my money," said Rufus. "If they do, I'll give 'em a rap with this."

The money was paid over, and the bat changed owners. It was heavy, and of hard wood, and in the hands even of a boy might prove a formidable weapon.

CHAPTER XXII.

A RESCUE.

ARMED with the bat, Rufus took his way up-town. As the distance was considerable, he jumped on board a horse-car. The conductor, noticing the bat, asked him whether he was going to play a game by moonlight.

"Yes," said the newsboy. "I belong to a club called 'The Owls.' We can play best in the dark."

He got out of the car at the point nearest to the place which he had heard mentioned as the probable scene of attack, and walked cautiously towards it. He had no doubt of being in full time, for it was not yet half-past eleven. But circumstances had hastened the attack; so that, as he turned the corner of a quiet side street, he was startled by seeing a gentleman struggling desperately in the hands of two ruffians.

He saw at a glance that they were the same he had overheard in the oyster saloon.

The gentleman appeared to be overpowered, for he was on the ground, with one man clutching his throat to prevent his giving the alarm, while the other was rifling his pockets.

There was no time to lose.

The newsboy darted forward, and before the villains were aware that their plans were menaced by defeat, he brought down the bat with force upon the back of the one who had his victim by the throat. The bat, wielded by the vigorous hand of Rough and Ready, fell with terrible emphasis upon the form of the bending ruffian. He released his hold with a sharp cry of pain, and fell back on the sidewalk. His companion looked up, but only in time to receive an equally forcible blow on his shoulder, which compelled him also to desist from his purpose.

At the same time the voice of the newsboy rang out clear and loud on the night air: "Help! Police!"

He sprang to the side of the prostrate gentleman.

saying, "Get up at once, sir. We'll defeat these villains yet."

The gentleman sprang to his feet, and prepared to do his part in resisting an attack; but none was apparently intended. The man, who had been struck in the back, was not in a position to do anything, but lay groaning with pain, while the other did not think it expedient to continue the attack under the changed aspect of affairs. Besides, the newsboy's cry for help was likely to bring the police, so that the only thing left was to effect an immediate escape.

He paused but an instant before making his decision; but that instant nearly destroyed his chance. The policeman, who had heard the cry for help, turned the corner hastily, and at once made chase. But by exerting all his strength the fellow managed to escape. The policeman returned, and began to inquire into the circumstances of the attack.

"How did this happen, Mr. Turner?" he inquired of the gentleman, whom he recognized.

"Those two villains attacked me," said the gentle

man, " just as I turned the corner. They must have
learned that I was likely to have a considerable sum
of money about me, and were planning to secure it.
Their attack was so sudden and unexpected tha
they would have accomplished their object but fo.
this brave boy."

" Curse him ! " said the prostrate burglar, who was
the shorter of the two. " I saw him in the oyster
saloon. He must have heard what I and my pal
were saying, and followed us."

" Did you know anything of this intended robbery ? " asked the policeman.

" Yes," said Rough and Ready, " the man is right.
I did overhear him and the other man planning it.
We were in an oyster saloon in the lower part of the
city. I was in one of the little rooms, and they in
the other. They were talking it over in a low voice ;
but I overheard the whole. As soon as I heard it, I
determined to stop it if I could. I had no weapon
with me, but was lucky enough to buy this bat of a
boy I met, and came up at once. I came near not
being in time."

" Let me see the bat," said the policeman.

" It's a tough customer," he said, weighing it in his hand; "you settled one of the parties, at any rate."

" Curse him! " muttered the burglar once more.

" Come, my man," said the policeman, " you must go with me. The city provides accommodations for such as you."

" I can't get up," he groaned.

"I guess you can if you try. You can't lie here, you know."

After some delay the man rose sullenly, groaning meanwhile.

" My back is broken," he said.

" I hope not," said the newsboy, who was moved with pity for the burglar, bad as he was.

" Don't pity him too much," said the policeman; " he deserves what he's got."

"I'll pay you off some time, boy, curse you! " said the injured man; with a vindictive glance at Rufus. " I'll give you as good as you gave."

" It'll be some time before you get a chance," said the policeman. " You'll get a five years in Sing Sing for this job."

He marched off with the culprit, and Rough and
Ready was left alone with Mr. Turner.

"I don't know how to thank you, my brave boy,
for your timely assistance," he said, grasping the
hand of the newsboy.

" I don't need any thanks, sir," said Rufus.

" You may not need any, but you deserve them
richly.   Are you far from home?"

" Yes, sir ; but I can take the horse-cars."

" Where do you live?"

" At the Newsboys' Lodging House."

" Are you a newsboy?" asked Mr. Turner, with
interest.

" Yes, sir."

" Have you parents living?"

" No, sir, except a stepfather ; but he's a drunkard,
and I don't live with him."

" Have you any brothers or sisters?"

" A little sister, about seven years old."

" Does she live with your stepfather?"

"I took her away, but Mr. Martin found out
where I had placed her, and he managed to get hold
of her.   I found out to-day where he carried her, and

to-morrow I shall try to get her back. He isn't a fit man to have the charge of her."

"And can you support your little sister, and your-self too?"

"Yes, sir."

"You are a good brother, and I believe you are a good boy. I want to know more of you. It is too late to go to the Newsboys' Lodging House to-night. I live close by, and will take you home with me."

"Thank you, sir," said Rough and Ready, bash-fully, "but I don't want to trouble you so much."

"There will be no trouble, and I owe something to a boy who has rendered me such a service. Besides, Mrs. Turner will want to see you."

The newsboy knew not what further objections to make, and, indeed, Mr. Turner gave him no time to think of any, for, placing his arm in his, he drew him along. His home was in the next block.

As Rufus ascended the steps, he saw that it was of fine appearance, and a new fit of bashfulness seized him. He wished himself in his accustomed bed at the Newsboys' Lodging House. There he would be under no constraint. Now he was about to enter a home where customs prevailed of which he knew nothing. But, whatever his feelings were, there was no chance to draw back. Besides, the alternative was between accepting Mr. Turner's invitation, and sleeping in the streets, for punctually at twelve o'clock the Lodging House closes, and it would be later than this before he could reach there.

Mr. Turner drew out a night-key, and opened the front door.

The hall was dimly lighted, for the gas was partially shut off. Still the newsboy could see that it was handsomely furnished. How it compared with other houses up-town he could not tell, for this was the first he had entered.

"The servants have gone to bed," said Mr. Turner; "I never require them to sit up after eleven. I will myself show you the room where you are to sleep. Your hat you may leave here."

According to directions, Rufus hung up his hat on the hat-stand. He congratulated himself, as he did so, that he had only bought it the week before, so that its appearance would do him no dis credit

Indeed his whole suit, though coarse, was whole, and not soiled, for he paid greater attention to dress than most boys in his line of business. This was due partly to a natural instinct of neatness, but partly also to the training he had received from his mother, who had been a neat woman.

"Now come upstairs with me, Rufus," said Mr. Turner, who had made himself acquainted with our hero's name. "I will ask you to step softly, that we may wake no one."

The thick carpet which covered the stairs rendered it easy to follow this direction.

"One more flight," said Mr. Turner, at the first landing.

He paused before a door on the third floor, and opened it.

Rufus followed him into a large and handsomely furnished bedchamber, containing a bed large enough for three, as the newsboy thought.

"I think you will find everything you need," said the master of the house, casting a rapid glance around. "I hope you will have a comfortable night's rest. We have breakfast at half-past seven ɔ'clock. The bell will ring to awake you half an hour earlier."

" I think I won't stop to breakfast," said Rough and Ready, bashfully ; " thank you, sir, for the invitation."

" You mustn't think of going away before breakfast," said Mr. Turner ; " I wish to talk with you, and my wife will wish to see you."

" But," said the newsboy, still anxious to get away, " I ought to be down-town early to get my papers."

" Let them go one morning. I will take care that you lose nothing by it. You will find a brush and comb on the bureau. And now, good-night. I am tired, and I have no doubt you are also."

" Good-night, sir."

The door closed, and the newsboy was left alone It had come so rapidly upon him, that he could hardly realize the novel circumstances in which he was placed. He, who had been accustomed to the humble lodgings appropriated to his class, found himself a welcome guest in a handsome mansion up-town. He undressed himself quickly, and, shutting off the gas, jumped into bed. He found it very soft and comfortable, and, being already fatigued, did not long remain awake, as he glided unconsciously into slumber, wondering vaguely what Ben Gibson would say if he knew where he was spending the night.

17

Rufus slept so soundly, that his slumber was only ended by the sound of the warning bell, at seven in the morning.

"Where am I?" he thought in bewilderment, as, opening his eyes, his first glance took in the appointments of the bedchamber.

Recollections quickly came to his aid, and, springing out of bed, he began to dress.

His feelings were rather mixed. He wished that he could glide softly downstairs, and out of the house, without stopping to breakfast. But this would not do, since Mr. Turner had expressly requested him to stay. But he dreaded meeting the rest of the family at the breakfast-table. He was afraid that he wouldn't know how to act in such unwonted circumstances, for, though bold enough, and ready enough in the company of boys and out in the street, he felt bashful in his present position.

He dressed himself slowly, and, finding a clothes-brush, brushed his clothes carefully. He arranged his hair neatly at the glass, which, though the news boy was not vain enough to suspect it, reflected the face and figure of a very attractive, and handsome boy.

When his preparations were all completed, he sat down in some perplexity. Should he go downstairs? He decided not to do so, for he did not know his way to the room where the family ate breakfast.

" I will wait till I hear the bell," he thought.

He had to wait ten or fifteen minutes, feeling some-what nervous the while.

At length the bell rang, and Rufus knew that it was time to go downstairs. He looked upon it as rather a trying ordeal, considering that he knew only the head of the family. Just as he was preparing to leave the room, the door was thrown open, and a boy of ten entered impetuously.

"Breakfast's ready," he said; "Pa-pa sent me up to show you the way."

" Thank you," said Rufus.

" What's your name?"

" Rufus."

" There's a boy in my class at school named Rufus, but he don't look much like you. Where's the
bat you knocked the robber down with?"

" Here," said the newsboy, smiling.

" I guess you gave him a crack, didn't you? I
wouldn't like to get hit with it. Do you play base
ball?"

" Not much."

" What do you want a bat for, then?"

" To knock robbers down," said Rufus, smiling.

" I belong to a base-ball club at school. We call
it the " Sea-Birds." We go up to the Park once a
week and play."

By this time they had reached the breakfast-room.
Mr. Turner, who was already down, advanced t
meet our hero, and took him by the hand.

" Did you sleep well, Rufus?" he said.

" Yes, sir. I only waked up when the bell
rung."

" It was late when we retired. Louisa, my dear,

this is the young lad who bravely came to my rescue when I was assaulted by two robbers."

Mrs. Turner, who was a pleasant-looking lady, took his hand cordially. " I am very glad my husband brought you home," she said. "I shudder to think what would have happened, if you had not come up. I shouldn't have minded the money; but he might have been killed. I don't see how you could have had the courage to attack them."

"I had a stout club," said Rufus ; " if it hadn't been for that, I couldn't have done any good."

" Nor would the club have done any good, if it hadn't been in the hands of a brave boy," said Mr. Turner. " But the breakfast is getting cold. Let us sit down."

Rufus took his seat in a chair indicated to him. He was glad to find that he was seated next to the boy, who had shown him the way downstairs, for with a boy he felt more at home than with an older person.

" What is your name?" he asked.

" Walter," was the reply. " I'm named after my

Uncle Walter. He's travelling in Europe. Are you in a store?"

"No."

"Do you go to school?"

"No, I sell papers. I'm a newsboy."

"Do you make much money?"

"About eight dollars a week."

"That's a good deal. I only get fifty cents a week for spending money."

"Which is twice as much as you ought to have," said his father. "I'm afraid you spend most of it for candy."

"I didn't know newsboys made so much money," said Walter.

"Rufus has a sister to support," said Mr. Turner. "You wouldn't think eight dollars much, if you had to pay all your expenses out of it, and support a sister besides."

"What is your sister's name?" asked Mrs. Turner.

"Rose."

"A very pretty name. How old is she?"

"Seven years old."

"That's just as old as my sister Carrie," said Walter; "here she comes. She's so lazy she always gets up late in the morning."

"No, I don't either," said the young lady referred to; "I'm not so lazy as you are, Master Walter."

"Well, then, why didn't you come down earlier?"

"Because I had to have my hair braided," said Carrie.

"Didn't I have to brush my hair?" said Walter.

"Your hair doesn't look as if you had spent much time on it," said his father.

"Pa-pa," said Walter, as he helped himself to a second piece of toast, "I wish you'd let me stop going to school, and sell papers."

"Do you think that would be a good plan?" asked his father, smiling.

"Yes, I could earn money, you know."

"Not much, I think. I suppose, if I agree to that arrangement, you will promise to pay all your expenses out of your earnings."

"Yes, I guess I could," said Walter, hesitating. "I can learn the business of Rufus."

"I don't think you'd like it very well," said our hero, amused.

"Don't you like it?"

"I don't think I should like to sell papers all my life."

"What are you going to do when you are a man?"

"I can't tell yet."

"By the way, Rufus, I should be glad to have you call at my counting-room, No. —— Wall Street, this morning."

"Thank you, sir," said Rufus; "but I should prefer to call to-morrow. This morning, I am going over to Brooklyn to see if I can recover my sister."

"To-morrow will answer just as well. Don't fail to come, however; I wish to have a talk with you about your prospects."

"I will not fail to come," answered the newsboy.

Rufus did not find it so embarrassing as he anticipated at the breakfast table. His young neighbor,

Walter, plied him with questions, many of which amused him, and occasionally his sister Carrie, on the opposite side of the table, joined in.   Mrs. Tur ner asked him questions about his little sister, and sympathized with him when he described the plot by which she had been taken from him.

" Do you know Latin? " inquired Walter.

" No," said Rufus.

" I don't see what's the use of studying it, for **my part.**   I never expect to talk Latin."

" I don't think you ever will," said his father; " judging from your school report, your success has not been very brilliant in that study, so far."

" I know one Latin sentence, anyway," said Walter, complacently.

" What is it? "

" *Sum stultus.*"

" I regret to hear it," said his father, in a tone of amusement.

" Why? " asked Walter, surprised.

" Do you understand the meaning of the words you have just used? "

" Yes, sir."

" Well, what is it? "

" They mean, ' I am good.' "

" Indeed, — I had an idea that their meaning was quite different.   Suppose you look out *stultus* in your dictionary."

" I am sure I am right," said Walter, confidently. " I will prove it to you."

He got his dictionary, and looked for the word He looked a little abashed when he found it.

" Well," said his father, " what does it mean? "

" I am a fool," returned Walter.

At this there was a laugh at Walter's expense. Breakfast was now over, and they rose from the table.

" I hope you will come and see us again," said Mrs. Turner.

" Thank you," said our hero.

" Come again, Rufus," said Walter ; " I'm making a boat, and perhaps you can help me.   I'd show it to you, only I've got to get ready to go to school.   I'm going to sail it in the bath-tub."

" I shall expect to see you at my office, to-mor-

row," said Mr. Turner, as Rufus took his leave.
"Don't forget the number, — Wall Street."

The door closed behind him, and Rufus descended
the steps. On the whole, he was glad now that
ne had remained to breakfast. It had not proved so
trying an ordeal as he anticipated, and he felt that
he had acquitted himself pretty well under the circumstances. It occurred to him that it would be
very pleasant to live in the same way if he could afford it; not that he cared so much for himself, but he
would like it if Rose could have the same advantages,
and live in as pleasant a home as Carrie Turner.

This recalled to his mind that Rose was still in the
power of his stepfather, and if he wished to secure
her it would be well to lose no time. He jumped on
a horse-car, and rode down-town. As he got out,
Ben Gibson, who had just finished a job, caught sight
of him.

"Why wasn't you at the Lodge last night?" he
asked.

"A gentleman invited me to stop at his house up
town."

"Oh, yes, of course," said Ben, incredulously

" It's true. But I want you to go over to Brooklyn with me, and show me just where Mr. Martin
lives. You shan't lose anything by it. I'll tell you
about my adventure last night, as we are walking
along."

" All right," said Ben ; " my health's getting delicate, and a trip to Brooklyn will be good for it."

Ben shouldered his box, and the two boys bent
their steps towards Fulton Ferry.

CHAPTER XXIV.

MR. MARTIN HAS AN IDEA.

WE must now return to Rose, whom we left con fined in the cellar. Now, a cellar is not a very pleas ant place, and Rose had a dismal time of it. She was considerably frightened also, when, as she sat on the lower step of the cellar stairs she saw a large rat running rapidly past. It is not to be wondered at that Rose was alarmed. I know many persons much older who would have done precisely what she did under the circumstances, namely, scream with all their might.

The little girl's scream brought Mrs. Waters to the door at the head of the stairs.

" What are you howling at? " she demanded, roughly.

" I just saw a big rat," said Rose. " Do let me come up ; I'm afraid he'll bite me."

" Most likely he will," said Mrs. Waters. " But I

can't let you come up. You've acted too bad. Next time you'll find it best to behave. And, mind you don't yell again! If you do, I'll come down and give you something to yell for."

Saying this, she slammed the door, and returned to her work, leaving Rose in a very unhappy state of mind. She sat in momentary expectation of the re-appearance of the rat, thinking it very likely it would bite her, as Mrs Waters had told her. She began to cry quietly, not daring to scream, lest Mrs. Waters should carry out her threat and give her a whipping.

At the end of an hour — it seemed more like a day to Rose — Mrs. Waters came to the door, and said, "You can come up now, if you can make up your mind to behave yourself."

Rose needed no second invitation. She ran up-stairs hastily, under the impression that the rat might pursue her, and breathed a sigh of relief when she was fairly out of danger.

Fanny was sitting at the table, eating a piece of apple-pie.

" Did the rats bite you? " she asked, laughing ma liciously.

" No," answered Rose.

" I wish they had. It would have been such fun to hear you holler."

" You're a mean girl," said Rose, indignantly.

" Hoity-toity ! What's all this?" demanded Mrs. Waters. " Have you begun to call Fanny names al ready?"

" She said she wished the rats had bitten me," said Rose.

" Well, so do I. It would have been a good lesson to you. Now, miss, I've got one word to say. If you abuse and quarrel with Fanny, I'll just put you down cellar again, and this time I'll keep you there all night. Do you hear?"

" Yes," said Rose, shuddering. She privately made up her mind that she should die if this threat were carried out, and the very thought of it made her turn pale.

" Don't you want some pie, Rose?" asked Fanny, with her mouth full.

" Yes," said Rose, " I should like some."

" Well, you can't have any," said Fanny, mali‧ ciously. " Can she, ma?"

"Of course not. She don't deserve any," said the mother. "Pie is too good for wicked girls. Here, you Rose, here's something for you to do, to keep you out of mischief. Sit down to the table here, and shell these beans. Don't you want to help, Fanny?"

"No, I don't," said Fanny, decidedly. "She can do 'em alone."

A tin-pan half full of bean-pods was placed on the table, and Rose was ordered to be " spry,". and not to waste her time. Fanny, having finished her pie, began to tease the cat, which employment she found much more satisfactory than helping Rose.

That night Mrs. Waters presented her bill to Mr. Martin for a week's board in advance for himself and Rose. The fact that he had apparently given up working made her a little doubtful whether he would prove good pay. She determined to ask payment in advance, and thus guard against all risk of loss.

"Mr. Martin," she said, " here's my bill for your board, and the little girl's. I'm rather short of money, and have got some bills to pay, and I should feel particularly obliged if you could pay me now."

Mr. Martin took the bill, and looked at it.

"It's seven dollars," said Mrs. Waters. "I can't afford to take any less. Beef's two cents a pound higher, and potatoes is rising every day. You can't say it's unreasonable."

"It's all right, Mrs. Waters," said Martin, slipping it into his vest-pocket. "It's all right. I'll attend to it in a day or two."

"Can't you pay me to-day?" persisted the landlady. "I've got my rent to pay to-morrow, and it'll take all I can get to pay it."

"Can you change a fifty-dollar bill?" asked Martin.

"I can get it changed."

"I guess I'll get it changed myself," said Martin. "I'm goin' out on business."

"I don't believe he's got so much money," thought Mrs. Waters, suspiciously, and it is needless to say that she was quite right in her suspicions. The exact amount of Mr. Martin's cash in hand was a dollar and thirty-seven cents, and his entire wardrobe and the sum of his earthly possessions would not probably have brought over fifteen dollars.

Strong as Mrs. Waters suspicions were, however,

18

she could not very well press the matter then. She
resolved to wait till Mr. Martin returned, and then
renew the subject. She would be guided in her
action by what happened then.

Martin, meanwhile, began to consider that possibly
he had made a mistake in kidnapping Rose. The
necessary outlay for her board and clothes would be
a serious drain upon him, especially as for years he
had barely earned enough to pay his own personal
expenses. On the whole, he thought he might as well
restore her to her brother ; but he would take care that
the newsboy paid for the concession. He thought he
might by good management get twenty dollars out
of him, or, if he had not so much, part down, and the
rest in a week or fortnight. He resolved to see Rough
and Ready about it the very next morning.

There are some who say that money earned is enjoyed the most. James Martin did not believe this.
Earning money was very disagreeable to him, and he
considered any other mode of getting it preferable.

He was lounging along the street, with his hands in
his pockets, meditating as above, when a little girl
came up to him, and, holding out her hand, whined

out, " Won't you give me a few pennies for my poor sick mother?"

Suddenly a brilliant idea came to Mr. Martin. He determined to question the little girl.

" How long have you been out beggin'?" he asked.

" Ever since morning."

" How much money have you made?"

The little girl hesitated.

" Come, little girl, if you'll tell me true, I'll give you five cents."

" I'll show you," she answered, regaining confidence.

She drew from her pocket a miscellaneous collection of pennies and silver pieces, which Martin counted, and found to amount to sixty-eight cents.

" Do you make as much every day, little gal?" he asked.

" Sometimes more," she answered.

" Pretty good business, isn't it? How long's your mother been sick?"

" Most a year," said the little girl, hesitating.

" What's the matter with her?"

" I don't know. She can't set up,"-said the girl, again hesitating, for she was a professional meudi-

cant, and the sick mother was a sham, being represented in reality by a lazy, able-bodied woman, who
spent most of the charitable contributions collected
by her daughter on drink.

"Oh, yes, I understand," said Martin, with a wink
"Good-by, little gal.   Give my love to your poor sick
mother, and tell her I'd come round and inquire after
her health if I had time."

As he said this he turned to go away.

"You promised me five cents," said the little girl
running after him.

"Did I?   Well, you'll have to wait till next time
unless you can change a fifty-dollar bill."

"I aint got money enough."

"Then you must wait till you see me again."

Mr. Martin's questions had not been without an
object.   The idea which had occurred to him was
this.   Why might he not make Rose, in like manner,
a source of income?   Perhaps he might in that way
more than pay expenses, and then he would still be
able to keep her, and so continue to spite Rough and
Ready, which would be very agreeable to his feelings.

"I'll send her out to-morrow morning," he said to

himself. "If she's smart, she can make a dollar a day, and that'll help along considerable. I'll be her poor sick mother. It'll save my workin' so hard, and njurin' my health in my old age."

The more Mr. Martin thought of this plan, the better he liked it, and the more he wondered that he had never before thought of making Rose a source of income.

CHAPTER XXV.

ROSE IS RESTORED TO HER BROTHER.

WHEN Mr. Martin re-entered his boarding-house late in the afternoon, Mrs. Waters looked as if she expected her bill to be paid.

" I couldn't change my fifty dollars," said Martin ; " but it's all right, Mrs. Waters. You shall have the money to-morrow."

Notwithstanding the confidence with which he spoke, Mrs. Waters felt rather troubled in mind. She doubted very much whether it was all right, and would have felt very much relieved if she could have seen the bank-note which Martin talked about changing. However, there was no good excuse for questioning his statement, and she could only wait as patiently as she might. But she resolved that if the money were not forthcoming the next day, she would advise Mr. Martin to seek another boarding-place, and that without delay.

When breakfast was over the next morning, Martin said to Rose, "Put on your bonnet. I want you to go out with me."

Rose looked at him in surprise.

"I'm goin' to get her some new clothes, ma'am," he said to Mrs. Waters. "She needs 'em, and it will give me a good chance to change my bill."

This might be so. Mrs. Waters hoped it was. Rose, however, listened with amazement. Her step-father had not bought her any clothes for years, — indeed, she could not remember when, — and it was not long since he had taken away and sold those which her brother bought her. The idea struck her with alarm that perhaps he had the same intention now.

"Come, don't be all day," said Martin, roughly. "Maybe I'll change my mind, and not buy you any if you're so long gettin' ready."

It took little time for Rose to make necessary preparations. After leaving the house, Mr. Martin led the way to Third Avenue, where they got on board the horse-cars. It struck Mr. Martin that a good place for Rose to commence her new profession would be in front of Fulton Ferry, where crowds of people were passing and repassing continually.

Rose did not venture to ask any questions till they reached their destination.

Then seeing the ferry, which she remembered, she asked hopefully, " Are we going to New York? "

" No, we aint. Don't you think of such a thing," said Martin, roughly.

" Are you going to buy me some clothes here? I don't see any stores."

" You've got clothes enough. You've got better clothes than I have."

" I thought," said Rose, " you told Mrs. Waters you were going to buy me some."

" Maybe I'll buy you some, if you do just as I tell you. I've got something for you to do."

They had now left the cars, and were crossing the street to the ferry.

" Now," said Martin, " I'll tell you what you must do. You must stand just there where people come out, and hold out your hand, and say, 'Give me a few pennies for my poor sick mother.'"

" But," said Rose, in dismay, " that will be begging."

" S'pose it is," retorted her stepfather, doggedly. " Are you too proud to beg? Do you expect me to support you without you doin' anything?"

" I'm willing to work," said Rose, " but I don't want to beg."

" None of your impudence l" said Martin, angrily. ".You must do just as I told you. Say, ' Give me a few pennies for my poor sick mother.' "

These last words he brought out in a doleful whine, such as he thought might excite compassion.

" There, see if you can say it as I did."

" I haven't got any sick mother," pleaded Rose.

" What's the odds? Half of them aint. Only you must say so, or they won't give you anything. Come, are you ready?"

" I don't want to beg," said Rose, desperately.

" I tell you what, little gal," said Martin, fiercely; " if you don't do as I tell you, I'll give you the wust lickin' you ever had. Say what I told you."

" Give me a few pennies for my poor sick mother," repeated Rose, unwillingly.

"You don't say it feelin' enough," said Martin, critically. "Anybody would think you didn't care nothin' for your poor sick mother. Say it so;" and he repeated the whine.

Rose said it after him, and though her performance was not quite satisfactory to her stepfather, he decided that it would do.

"There, stand there," he said, "and begin. I'm goin' just across the street, and if you don't do it right, look out for a lickin'."

Rose took her position, feeling very much ashamed, and almost ready to cry. She wished she could escape the necessity; but looking across the street she saw Martin furtively shaking his fist at her, and turned desperately to follow his directions.

The boat was just in, and a throng of passengers was passing through the gate.

"Give me a few pennies for my poor sick mother," said Rose, to a good-natured-looking man who passed her.

He looked at her anxious face, and something in it excited his pity. He took out ten cents, and gave it to her. Rose took it, feeling very much ashamed, and turned to the next passer.

"Give me a few pennies for my poor sick moth er," she said.

"Out of the way there, you young beggar!" said he, roughly. "Such nuisances as you are ought to be sent to the Island."

Rose drew back alarmed at this rough language, and for a moment kept silent, hardly daring to re-new her appeal. But a look at James Martin's threatening face compelled her to continue, and again she made the appeal.

This time it was a lady she addressed, — mild and pleasant, — who paused a moment, and spoke gently.

"Is your mother quite sick, my dear?" she asked, in a voice of compassion.

"Yes, ma'am," answered Rose, faintly, ashamed of the falsehood she was uttering.

"Have you any brothers and sisters?"

"One brother," answered Rose, glad that here at least she could tell the truth.

"Here's something for you," said the lady, placing twenty-five cents in the child's outstretched palm.

All the passengers had now passed through the portal, and she had some respite.

James Martin crossed the street, and, coming up to her, asked, " How much did you get? "

Rose opened her hand.

" Thirty-five cents in five minutes," he said, elated " Come, little gal, you're gettin' on finely. I snouldn't wonder if you'd take three or four dollars by two o'clock. We'll go home then."

" But I don't like to beg," said Rose.

" Don't let me hear none of that," said Martin, angrily. " You're lazy, that's what's the matter. You've got to earn your livin', there's no two ways about that, and this is the easiest way to do it. There aint no work about beggin'."

Since Martin was mean enough to live on the money begged by a little girl, it isn't likely that he would understand the delicate scrupulousness which made Rose ashamed of soliciting charity.

" I'll take the money," said her stepfather, " and you can get some more when the next boat comes in. I'm goin' away a few minutes," he proceeded ; " but you must stay here just where you are, and keep on just as if I was here. I won't be gone long. If I find you haven't done nothing when I come back, look out for yourself."

James Martin had reflected that the thirty-five cents would be sufficient to get him a drink and a couple of cigars, and it was to obtain these that he went away. He found it rather dull work, standing on the sidewalk and watching Rose, and he thought that by inspiring her with a little wholesome fear, she would go on just as well in his absence. Still it might be as well to encourage her a little.

" If you're a good gal," he proceeded, in a changed tone, " and get a lot of money, I'll buy you some candy when we go home."

This, however, did not cheer Rose much. She would much prefer to go without the candy, if she might be relieved from her present disagreeable employment.

If Mr. Martin had been aware that among the passengers on the next boat were Rough and Ready and Ben Gibson, he would scarcely have felt so safe in leaving Rose behind. Such, however, was the case. While Rose was plunged in sorrowful thought, filled with shame at the thought of her employment, deliverance was near at hand.

The boat came in, and she felt compelled to resume her appeal.

" Give me a few pennies for my poor sick mother," she said, holding out her hand.

" Where is your poor sick mother?" asked the person addressed.

" She's dead," said Rose, forgetting herself.

" That's what I thought," he answered, laughing, and passed on, of course without giving anything.

Rather mortified at the mistake she had made, Rose turned to address the next passenger, when she uttered a joyful cry.

" O Rufie !" she exclaimed, throwing her arms around him.

" Rose, is it you?" he exclaimed, surprised and delighted. "How came you here? I came over to Brooklyn on purpose to find you ; but I had no idea you were so near."

" Mr. Martin sent me here to beg."

' To beg !" repeated Rufus, indignantly. " And where is he now ? "

" He's gone away," said Rose, " but he's coming right back."

" Then he won't find you, that's all. Come, Ben we'll go right back by the next boat, and carry Rose with us. I didn't expect to be so lucky."

" Won't Martin be mad?" said Ben. " I'd like to see him when he finds your sister gone."

" He shan't see her again very soon," said Rufus, " not if I can help it. Come along, Rose."

He paid their fare by the boat, and hurried Rose on board. It started in the course of two or three minutes on its return trip. On the way he made Rose tell him how she had been treated, and was very angry when told of the persecutions to which she had been subjected.

" But it's all over now, Rosy," he said, putting his arm caressingly round his little sister's neck, " you're safe now, and nobody shall trouble you. Miss Manning will be rejoiced to see you again."

" I shall be *so* glad to get home again, Rufie," said Rose, earnestly ; " Miss Manning's so much nicer than Mrs. Waters."

"And am I as nice as Mr. Martin?" asked Rufus, laughing.

"Ten thousand million times," said Rose, emphat-cally. "He isn't nice at all."

Meanwhile we return to Mr. Martin.

When he got back, he looked in vain for Rose.

"Where's she gone?" he asked himself, angrily.

He looked about him on all sides, but no Rose was to be seen. It occurred to him that perhaps she might have taken some of the money obtained by begging, and gone over to New York in the boat, in the hope of finding her brother. If so, he would fol-low her.

To make sure, he asked the fare-taker.

"Did you see a little girl begging just outside the gate a few minutes ago?"

"Yes."

"She's gone away. Did you see where she went?"

"She went over to New York in the boat, about twenty minutes ago."

"Did she go alone?"

"No ; there were two boys went with her."

Martin asked for a description of the boys, and re
alized to his intense disappointment that his plans
were foiled, and that Rough and Ready had recovered
his sister. He was provoked with himself for leaving
her, and his vexation was the greater that he had not
only lost Rose and the money she might have made
for him, but also the sum which the newsboy stood
ready to pay for the return of his sister.

"Confound the luck!" he muttered. "It's always
against me"

CHAPTER XXVI.

CONCLUSION.

"Now," said Rufus, "we'll surprise Miss Manning. She won't be expecting you."

"Do you think Mr. Martin will come after me, Rufie?" asked Rose, anxiously.

"If he does he won't get you."

"I shan't dare to go out in the street."

"You had better not go out alone. I'll tell Miss Manning about it. I think it will be best to move to some other street, as long as Mr. Martin knows the old place."

"Maybe he'd like to adopt me instead of Rose," suggested Ben, humorously. "I'd make an interestin'-lookin' girl if I could only borrer a dress that would fit me."

"You'd have to give up smoking, Ben. Girls don't smoke."

"I'm afraid that wouldn't agree with me." said Ben,

" I guess Mrs. Waters would find you a tough customer, if she undertook to shut you up in the cel
lar."

" Yes," said Ben, " she'd find me as tough as a
ten-year-old turkey."

At Printing House Square, Ben left the party, and
resumed his professional occupation. As he will
not again be mentioned in this story, I will mention
that an account of his subsequent career may be found
in " Mark, the Match Boy," the third volume of this
series.

Miss Manning was sitting in her humble room
sewing diligently. She was thinking sadly how
cheerless and lonely it was since Rose had disappeared. She was not very sanguine about recovering
her, since it was much easier to hide a little girl than
to find her among such a wilderness of houses as the
great city contains. But, as she sat at her work, a
sound of footsteps was heard upon the stairs, and directly afterwards the door flew open, and little Rose,
rushing forward, threw her arms around her neck.

" Have you come back again, Rose?" exclaimed
the seamstress, joyfully.

"Yes, Miss Manning, I'm so glad to see you again;" and Rose kissed her again and again.

"How did you find her, Rufus?" asked Miss Manning, returning the embrace.

The newsboy related the story briefly.

Then Rose was called upon to give an account of all that had happened to her.

"What a wicked woman Mrs. Waters must be!" said the mild seamstress, with a display of indignation unusual for her. "She ought to be ashamed of herself to shut you up in a dark cellar."

"I was so afraid of the rats," said Rose, shuddering. "I was afraid they would eat me up."

"You'd make a pretty large mouthful for a common-sized rat," said Rufus, smiling.

"They might have bitten me, though," said Rose.

"Well, they shan't trouble you any more, little sister," said Rufus. "Mr. Martin will be a smart man if he gets hold of you again."

"He might carry *you* off, Rufie," said Rose, in momentary alarm.

"I'd like to see him do it," said Rough and Ready.

drawing up his youthful form. "He'd wish he hadn't, that's all," he added, with a laugh.

"I think, Miss Manning," he proceeded, "we'd better move, so as to put Martin off the track. As long as Rose lives here, he'll be prowling round, and some time he might get hold of her again."

"I am perfectly willing," said the seamstress. "My week's up to-morrow, and I can move at once. Suppose we go out and find a place this afternoon."

"All right," said Rufus. "But I've got to leave you now. I've a business engagement down in Wall Street."

"Among the bulls and bears," said Miss Manning, smiling.

"Are there bulls and bears in Wall Street?" said Rose, alarmed. "Oh, don't go down there, Rufie. You'll get killed."

"They won't hurt me, Rose. I haven't got money enough," said the newsboy, smiling. "Don't be afraid. I'll come back early in the afternoon."

The newsboy took the nearest route to Wall Street. It is a short street; but an immense volume of business is transacted there every day It is lined with banks and business offices, especially those of brokers, lawyers, insurance companies, and moneyed institutions. There were plenty of bulls and bears upon the street; but they looked very much alike. and Rufus could not tell them apart.

As these terms may seem mysterious to some of my young readers, it may be as well to say that " bulls " are those who are striving to carry up the price of stocks, and " bears " are those who are making an effort to depress them.

Our hero was not long in finding the office of Mr. Turner.

He had to go up a short flight of steps, at the head of which a door opened into a hall or entry-way. On one side of this was the office of Mr. Turner. Opening the office-door, he found himself in a large room fitted up with a counter, behind which were two or three young men, who were, no doubt, clerks.

" Is Mr. Turner in? " asked the newsboy, going up to the counter.

" Not just now; he's at the Board," — meaning the Stock Board, where stocks are bought and sold. " Can I do your business? "

" No ; Mr. Turner asked me to call.''

" You can wait for him, if you like."

Rough and Ready sat down in an arm-chair, and took up the morning paper. He had been thus engaged about twenty minutes, when he heard the door open, and, looking up, saw Mr. Turner.

" Good-morning, Mr. Turner," said our hero, laying aside the paper, and rising.

" Oh, good-morning, Rufus. I am glad to see you. Wait a few minutes, and I will be at leisure."

He went behind the counter, and gave a few quick business directions to his clerks.

" James, go to the Park Bank, and get these shares transferred to John Wade," he said to the youngest clerk, who thereupon seized his hat and left the office.

It was not long before Mr. Turner was disengaged Coming out from behind the counter, he drew up an arm-chair, and sat down opposite Rufus.

" So you are a newsboy?" he said.

" Yes, sir."

" But you don't want to be a newsboy always?"

" No, sir," said Rufus, promptly. " Only there

isn't much chance for me to get anything better to do."

"How much do you earn by selling papers?"

"About eight dollars a week."

"And out of that you support your sister and yourself?"

"Yes, sir."

"I suppose you have not been able to lay up any money."

"Yes, sir."

"How much?"

"Three hundred dollars."

"Three hundred dollars!" repeated Mr. Turner, in surprise. "Surely you could not save up so much as that?"

"No, sir, I found it."

"Tell me about it."

Our hero told of his adventure in the bar-room.

"So you have not spent any of this money?"

"No, sir; I put it in the savings-bank."

"That is well," said the broker, approvingly. "It shows that you have more good sense than most boys of your class. Now I have a proposition to make to you. How should you like to enter this office?"

"I should like it very much, sir."

"Better than being a newsboy?"

"Yes, sir; there aint any chance to rise in the paper business."

"And here, if you do your duty, there will be a chance to rise."

"Yes, sir, that's what I mean."

"Very well, I will tell you what I will do. You did me a signal service last night. You saved me from losing a large sum of money, and, what is worse from serious personal injury. I want to do something for you in return. I think you are a smart boy, and, what is better, an honest and trustworthy boy. It so happens that my youngest clerk is in poor health, and is about to leave my employment I will give you his place."

"Thank you, sir," said Rufus.

"As to salary I shall for the present give you the same you have been earning by selling papers, — that is, eight dollars a week. It is nearly double what I have been accustomed to pay, but that is of no con

sequence.   Besides this, I will give you two hundred
dollars to add to your fund in the savings-bank, in-
creasing it to five hundred."

"You are very, very kind," said Rufus.

"I owe you some kindness," said Mr. Turner.
"There are other ways in which I shall find an opportunity to serve you.   But of that we will speak hereafter.   When do you want to come?"

"Whenever you think best, sir."

"Then let it be next Monday morning, at nine
o'clock.   James will remain a week or two, till you
get a little familiar with your duties.   And now, my
young friend, this is all the time I can spare you this
morning.   Good-by till Monday."

Mr. Turner shook hands with Rufus, and the latter
left the office with the strange feeling which we always
have when a great change is going to take place in
our course of life.   He was about to bid farewell to
the life of a newsboy, and enter upon a business
career in Wall Street.   He could not help feeling a
thrill of new importance as he thought of this, and
his ambition was roused.   Why should he not rise
to a position of importance like the men whom he had

heard of and seen, whose beginnings had been as humble as his own? He determined to try, at all events.

He returned to Miss Manning to acquaint her and Rose with his good fortune. The seamstress seemed quite impressed with the news.

" Who knows what may come of it, Rufus?" she said. " Some day you may be a rich man, — perhaps president of a bank."

" Which shall 1 be, Rose, a bull or a bear?" inquired Rufus, playfully.

" You can't be a bull," said Rose, positively, " foi you haven't got any horns."

" Then I suppose I must be a bear," said the newsboy, laughing.

So Rufus ceased to be a newsboy, and here appropriately closes the story of " ROUGH AND READY ; or, Life among the New York Newsboys." But a new career dawns upon our hero, brighter than the past, but not without its trials and difficulties. Those who are interested to hear of his new life, and are curious to learn what became of Mr. Martin, will find the account given in a subsequent volume, for next Christ mas, to be called "RUFUS AND ROSE; or, *The Adventures of Rough and Ready.*" Before writing this, however, I propose to publish, as the next volume of this series, the experiences of one of the newsboy's friends, under the title of

BEN, THE LUGGAGE BOY;

or,

AMONG THE WHARVES.

Famous Castlemon Books.

No author of the present day has become a greater favorite with boys than "Harry Castlemon," every book by him is sure to meet with-hearty reception by young readers generally. His naturalness and vivacity leads his readers from page to page with breathless interest, and when one volume is finished the fascinated reader, like Oliver Twist, asks "for more"

By Harry Castlemon.

GUNBOAT SERIES. By Harry Castlemon. In box containing the following. 6 vols. 16mo. Cloth, extra, black and gold $7 50
(Sold separately)

Frank the Young Naturalist. Illustrated. 16mo.   1 25

Frank in the Woods. Illustrated. 16mo. 1 25

Frank on the Prairie. Illustrated. 16mo. 1 25

Frank on a Gunboat. Illustrated. 16mo 1 25

Frank before Vicksburg. Illustrated. 16mo. . . 1 25

Frank on the Lower Mississippi. Illustrated. 16mo. 1 25

GO AHEAD SERIES. By Harry Castlemon. In box containing the following 3 vols. 16mo. Cloth, extra, black and gold 3 75
(Sold separately.)

Go Ahead; or, The Fisher Boy's Motto. Illustrated. 16mo. **$1 25**

No Moss; or, The Career of a Rolling Stone. Illustrated. 16mo. 1 25

Tom Newcombe; or, The Boy of Bad Habits. Illustrated. 16mo. 1 25

ROCKY MOUNTAIN SERIES. By Harry Castlemon. In box containing the following. 3 vols. 16mo Cloth, extra, black and gold . . . . 3 75 (Sold separately)

Frank at Don Carlos' Rancho. Illustrated. 16mo. 1 25

Frank among the Rancheros. Illustrated. 16mo. 1 25

Frank in the Mountains. Illustrated. 16mo . . 1 25

SPORTSMAN'S CLUB SERIES. By Harry Castlemon. In box containing the following. 3 vols. 16mo. Cloth, extra, black and gold . . . . 3 75 (Sold separately)

The Sportsman's Club in the Saddle. Illustrated. 16mo. Cloth, extra, black and gold 1 25

The Sportsman's Club Afloat. Being the 2d volume of the " Sportsman's Club Series " Illustrated. 16mo. Cloth, extra, black and gold 1 25

The Sportsman's Club among the Trappers. Being the 3d volume of the "Sportsman's Club Series." Illustrated. 16mo Cloth, extra, black and gold 1 25

FRANK NELSON SERIES. By Harry Castlemon In box containing the following. 3 vols. 16mo. Cloth, extra, black and gold . . . . 3 75 (Sold separately.)

Snowed up; or, The Sportsman's Club in the Mountains. Illustrated. 16mo 1 25

Frank Nelson in the Forecastle; or, the Sportsman's Club among the Whalers Illustrated. 16mo. 1 25

The Boy Traders; or, The Sportsman's Club among the Boers. Illustrated. 16mo 1 25

BOY TRAPPER SERIES. By Harry Castlemon. In box containing the following 3 vols. 16mo. Cloth, extra, black and gold **$3 75**
   (Sold separately)

The Buried Treasure; or, Old Jordan's "Haunt" Being the 1st volume of the "Boy Trapper Series." Illustrated. 16mo. **1 25**

The Boy Trapper; or, How Dave filled the Order. Being the 2d volume of the "Boy Trapper Series" Illustrated. 16mo. **1 25**

The Mail Carrier. Being the 3d and concluding volume of the "Boy Trapper Series." Illustrated. 16mo. **1 25**

ROUGHING IT SERIES. By Harry Castlemon. In box containing the following. 3 vols. Cloth, extra, black and gold **3 75**
   (Sold separately)

George in Camp; or, Life on the Plains. Being the 1st volume of the "Roughing It Series" Illustrated. 16mo. **1 25**

George at the Wheel; or, Life in a Pilot House Being the 2d volume of the ' Roughing It Series." Illustrated. 16mo **1 25**

George at the Fort; or, Life Among the Soldiers. Being the 3d and concluding volume of the "Roughing It Series." Illustrated. 16mo. **1 25**

ROD AND GUN SERIES. By Harry Castlemon. In box containing the following 3 vols. Cloth, extra, black and gold **3 75**
   (Sold separately).

Don Gordon's Shooting Box. Being the 1st volume of the "Rod and Gun Series" Illustrated. 16mo. **1 25**

Rod and Gun. Being the second volume of the "Rod and Gun Series" Illustrated. 16mo. . . . **1 25**

The Young Wild Fowlers. Being the third volume of the "Rod and Gun Series." Illustrated. 16mo. **1 25**

Alger's Renowned Books.

Horatio Alger, Jr , has attained distinction as one of the most popular writers of books for boys, and the following list comprises all of his best books

~~~~~~~~~~

By Horatio Alger, Jr.

RAGGED DICK SERIES. By Horatio Alger, Jr , in box containing the following. 6 vols. 16mo. Cloth, extra, black and gold . . . . **$7 50** (Sold separately)

Ragged Dick; or, Street Life in New York. Illustrated. 16mo. 1 25

Fame and Fortune; or, The Progress of Richard Hunter Illustrated. 16mo 1 25

Mark the Match Boy; or, Richard Hunter's Ward. Illustrated 16mo. 1 25

Rough and Ready; or, Life among the New York Newsboys. Illustrated. 16mo. 1 25

Ben the Luggage Boy; or, Among the Wharves. Illustrated. 16mo 1 25

Rufus and Rose; or, The Fortunes of Rough and Ready. Illustrated. 16mo 1 25

TATTERED TOM SERIES. (FIRST SERIES) By Horatio Alger, Jr , in box containing the following. 4 vols 16mo Cloth, extra, black and gold . . . 5 00 (Sold separately)

Tattered Tom; or, The Story of a Street Arab Illustrated 16mo. 1 25

Paul the Peddler; or, The Adventures of a Young Street Merchant. Illustrated. 16mo 1 25

Phil the Fiddler; or, The Young Street Musician. Illustrated. 16mo. 1 25

CPSIA information can be obtained
at www.ICGtesting.com
Printed in the USA
LVOW13s1024020617
536727LV00018B/325/P